Greek Paradise Escape

Travel from the comfort of your armchair with
Jennifer Faye's latest trilogy!

Nestled on a private Greek Island, the exclusive
Ludus Resort is the perfect escape for the rich and
famous. But to the staff who work there, it's home.

Manager Hermione's job has been a lifeline since
losing her home and family, so when new owner
Atlas plans to sell, sparks fly between them!

Beach artist Indigo is new to the resort and has
already caught the eye of one of its VIP guests, the
Prince of Rydiania...

Concierge Adara spends her days fulfilling guests'
wishes. Might it be time her own romantic dreams
came true?

Make your escape to beautiful Ludus in

Greek Heir to Claim Her Heart
and
It Started with a Royal Kiss

And continue your journey with Adara's story,
coming soon!

Dear Reader,

Sometimes thoughts are instilled in our minds from an early age and it can be difficult to overcome those beliefs in order to find our own truth. Such is the case for both my hero and heroine.

Artist Indigo Castellanos's life has faced much turmoil. And now, in order to provide for her ailing mother, she's taken a position at the Ludus Resort, where she runs into Prince Istvan. Her father had warned her not to trust a Rydianian royal. But he never mentioned how the prince could be so charming and persistent.

Prince Istvan of Rydiania is on Ludus Island for the royal regatta. He's convinced his destiny is preordained. And then he latches on to the idea of hiring Indigo to paint his formal portrait. Her fresh approach will be a visual reminder of the change he intends to bring to the kingdom.

Under normal circumstances, this job would be a dream come true—if only this prince's family hadn't ruined her father's life. However, Indigo can't afford to turn down Prince Istvan's generous offer. But when he discovers her true identity, will it ruin any chance of happiness for them?

Happy reading!

Jennifer

It Started with a Royal Kiss

Jennifer Faye

HARLEQUIN

Romance

HARLEQUIN®
Romance™

Recycling programs
for this product may
not exist in your area.

ISBN-13: 978-1-335-73674-1

It Started with a Royal Kiss

Harlequin Enterprises ULC
22 Adelaide St. West, 41st Floor
Toronto, Ontario M5H 4E3, Canada
www.Harlequin.com

Printed in U.S.A.

Award-winning author **Jennifer Faye** pens fun, heartwarming contemporary romances with rugged cowboys, sexy billionaires and enchanting royalty. Internationally published, with books translated into nine languages, she is a two-time winner of the *RT Book Reviews* Reviewers' Choice Award. She has also won the CataRomance Reviewers' Choice Award, been named a Top Pick author and been nominated for numerous other awards.

Books by Jennifer Faye

Harlequin Romance

Greek Paradise Escape

Greek Heir to Claim Her Heart

Wedding Bells at Lake Como

Bound by a Ring and a Secret
Falling for Her Convenient Groom

The Bartolini Legacy

The Prince and the Wedding Planner
The CEO, the Puppy and Me
The Italian's Unexpected Heir

Her Christmas Pregnancy Surprise
Fairytale Christmas with the Millionaire

Visit the Author Profile page
at Harlequin.com for more titles.

CHAPTER ONE

A PRINCE.

A genuine, sexy-as-all-get-out royal prince.

Indigo Castellanos swallowed hard. She couldn't believe she'd come face-to-face with Prince Istvan of Rydiania. She didn't want to be impressed—not at all—but she couldn't deny being a little bit awed by his mesmerizing blue eyes and tanned face. Just the memory of his shirtless body sent her traitorous heart racing.

She never in a million years thought they'd actually meet. When she'd taken this artist position at the Ludus Resort, she'd known the prince had ties to the private island. Still, it was a large resort—big enough to avoid certain people. Sure, the royal regatta was going on, but she'd mistakenly thought the prince would be too busy to attend. And if he did make an appearance, he wouldn't meander around the resort like some commoner.

And then, when she did meet him, she hadn't said a word. If staring into his bottomless eyes hadn't been bad enough, she'd been stunned into silence by his muscled chest and trim waist.

She gave herself a mental shake. None of that mattered. Not at all.

Nothing changed the fact that the prince came from the same family that had cast her father out of his homeland. But she didn't have time to think of that now. Besides, she didn't expect to see the prince again.

She perched on a stool beneath a great big red umbrella. Her bare, painted toes wiggled in the warm sand. She was so thankful for this job. It helped her care for her ailing mother. And she would do anything for her mother.

"Is she sitting in the right position?"

The woman's voice drew Indigo from her thoughts. She focused on the mother and young daughter in front of her. The girl was seated on a stool. "Um, yes. Why?"

"Because you were frowning." The mother didn't look happy.

"So sorry. Your daughter is just perfect." Indigo forced a reassuring smile to her lips. "The glare off the water is making it hard to see."

Indigo shifted her position on the stool. She couldn't afford to have her clients think she wasn't happy or they wouldn't continue to bring their children and family members to have her draw caricatures of them. And without the clients there would be no job—without a job, she wouldn't be able to pay the mounting medical bills.

She forced herself to concentrate on her work. Her art was what had gotten her through the tough times in her life, from her father's sudden death to her mother's collapse. Whereas some people lived charmed lives—Prince Istvan's handsome image came to mind—other people were not so fortunate. She didn't let the challenges stop her from striving for something better—from believing if she just kept trying, good things were awaiting her.

Minutes later, she finished the young girl's caricature and gently unclipped the paper from her easel. She handed it over to the mother, who didn't smile as she examined Indigo's work. She then held it out to her nine-year-old daughter and asked her opinion. The girl's eyes widened as a big smile puffed up her cheeks. And that was all Indigo needed to make her day. After all, it was as her father used to say: *it's the small things in life where you find the greatest reward.*

"Wait until I show my friends."

"Now what do you say?" the mother prompted.

The girl turned her attention to Indigo. "Thank you."

"You're welcome." In that moment, it didn't matter that Indigo was doing fun sketches instead of grand works of art. The only thing that mattered was that she'd brought some happiness to this girl's life.

"May I see it?" a male voice asked.

Indigo turned her head, and once again, she was caught off guard by the handsome prince. Her heart started to pitter-patter as she stared at him. What were the chances of them accidentally running into each other again?

"Oh." The mother's hand flew to her chest. "Your Highness." The woman did a deep curtsy.

The young girl's eyes filled with confusion as her gaze moved between her mother and Prince Istvan. Then her mother gestured for her to do the same thing. While the girl did a semi curtsy, Indigo sat by and took in the scene.

Was the prince here to see the mother? Did they have some sort of business together? Because there was absolutely no way he was there to see her. Not a chance. The royals and the Castellanos no longer intermingled—by royal decree. The reminder set Indigo's back teeth grinding together.

The prince turned in her direction. His eyes widened in surprise. Was it because he wasn't expecting to run into her again so soon? Or was it that she wasn't falling all over herself in front of him doing a curtsy? She refused to bow to him.

She should say something, but her mouth had gone dry. Words lodged in the back of her throat. And her heart was beating out of control. What was wrong with her?

The prince turned his attention back to the drawing. "It's fabulous. And who would the pretty young woman in the drawing be?"

"That's me," the girl said proudly.

The prince made a big deal of holding the sketch up next to the young girl, and then his dark brows drew together as his gaze moved between her and the drawing. "So it is. You're lucky to have such a lovely sketch." He returned the paper to the girl. "Enjoy your day."

The mother and daughter curtsied again. Then the mother reached in her bright orange-and-white beach bag. She withdrew her phone. With the consent of the prince, she took a selfie with him. Though the prince smiled for the picture, Indigo noticed how the smile did not go the whole way to his blue eyes.

After the woman repeatedly thanked him, she turned to Indigo. "How much do I owe you?"

"Nothing," Indigo said. "It's a courtesy of the resort."

"Oh." She dropped her phone in her bag. "Thank you." And then her attention returned to the prince. She curtsied again.

Indigo wondered if she'd looked that ridiculous the other day when she'd first met the prince. She hoped not. But she had been totally caught off guard.

She expected him to move on, but he didn't. His attention turned to her. "And so we meet again."

She swallowed hard. "Your Highness."

Quite honestly, she didn't know what to say to him. He certainly didn't want to hear anything she had to say about him or his family—about how they were cold and uncaring about whom they hurt in the name of the crown. No, it was best not to go there. She didn't think her boss would approve of her vocalizing her true feelings about the prince's family.

She glanced down at the blank page in front of her. She could feel the prince's gaze upon her. What was he thinking? Did he recognize her?

Impossible. She'd only been a very young child when her family had fled Rydiania. Back then she'd been scared and confused. She'd had no idea why they were leaving their home and everything they'd ever known to move to Greece— a land that she'd never visited, filled with people she did not know.

"Shall I sit here?" The prince's deep voice drew her from her troubled thoughts.

"If you like." In an effort not to stare at his tanned chest, she barely glanced at him. Though it was a huge temptation. Very tempting indeed. Instead she fussed over the blank sheet of paper on her easel, pretending to straighten it.

What did he want? Surely he wasn't going to take the time to flirt with her when she had no standing in his regal world. So if he wasn't there to flirt with her, why was he lingering?

Curiosity got the best of her. "Is there something I can do for you?"

He smiled at her, but the happiness didn't show in his eyes. It was though there was something nagging at him that he didn't want to share with her. She wondered what could weigh so heavily on a prince's mind.

"I would like you to draw me."

Her gaze lifted just in time to witness him crossing his arms over that perfectly sculpted chest. *Oh, my!* The breath stilled in her chest as she continued to drink in the sight of his tanned and toned body. She wondered if he spent all his free time in the gym. Because there was no way anyone looked as good as him without working at it.

Her attention slipped down over the corded muscles of his arms and landed on his six-pack abs. It wasn't until her gaze reached the waistband of his blue-and-white board shorts that she realized she shouldn't be staring.

"Will that be a problem?" His voice drew her attention back to his face.

This time when she stared into his eyes, she noticed a hint of amusement twinkling in his eyes. She'd been totally busted staring at him. Heat started in her chest and worked its way up her neck. What was she doing, checking out the enemy?

Just keep it together. You need to keep this job.

Her little pep talk calmed her down just a bit. She drew in a deep breath and slowly released it.

"Surely you have better things to do—erm, more important things than to have me sketch you."

She couldn't believe she was brushing off an opportunity to sketch a prince. If her friends could see her now they'd probably rush her to the hospital, certain she'd lost her grip on reality. But Istvan wasn't just any prince.

"I'm right where I want to be. Go ahead. Draw me."

Indigo hesitated. If he was anyone else but a member of the Rydianian royal family, she'd have jumped at the opportunity.

She'd grown up hearing stories of how the royal family wasn't to be trusted—that they put the crown above all else, including love of family. Her father was never the same after the former king, Georgios, and those in service to him were cast out of the kingdom. How could they do something so heartless?

"Is there a problem?" The prince's gaze studied her.

Unless she wanted to reveal the truth and put her new position at the Ludus Resort in jeopardy, she'd best get on with her job. She just had to pretend he was like any other guest at the resort, but she feared she wasn't that good of an actress.

She swallowed hard. "I don't think my sketch would do you justice."

He arched a brow. "Are you refusing to draw me?"

She thought about it. How many times had this

prince been denied something he wanted? She doubted it ever happened. Oh, how she'd like to be the first to do it. But even she wasn't that reckless.

"No." She grabbed her black brush pen. Then her gaze rose to meet his. "I just want you to understand that it won't be a conservative, traditional portrait."

"I understand. And I don't want it to be. Just pretend I'm any other patron." He settled himself on the stool while his security staff fanned out around him.

He was most definitely not just any other person—not even close. And yet he didn't have a clue who she was or how his family had destroyed hers. She thought of telling him, but what would that accomplish?

As she lifted her hand to the page, she noticed its slight tremor. She told herself she could do this. After all, the sooner she finished the sketch, the sooner the prince would move on. And so she pressed the brush pen to the paper and set to work.

It was impossible to do her job without looking at him. Her fingers tingled with the temptation to reach out to the dark, loose curls scattered over the top of his head. The sides and back of his head were clipped short. His tanned face had an aristocratic look, with a straight nose that wasn't too big nor too small. Dark brows highlighted his intense blue eyes with dark lashes. And a close-trimmed mustache and goatee framed his kiss-able lips.

In order to do her job, she had to take in every tiny detail of the person in front of her and translate them onto paper. And normally that wasn't hard for her. But sketching the prince was going to be the biggest challenge of her career as her heart raced and her fingers refused to cooperate.

She glanced around at the finely dressed men with hulking biceps and dark sunglasses. They were facing away from Istvan and Indigo, as though they were giving them some privacy while protecting them from the rest of the world.

"Don't worry about them," Prince Istvan said as though he could read her thoughts. "They're here to make sure there are no unwanted disturbances."

Indigo kept moving the black brush pen over the page. On second thought, the prince was really a pleasure to sketch with his strong jawline and firm chin. And then there was the dimple in his left cheek. Under any other circumstances, she'd readily admit that he was the most handsome man she'd ever sketched. But she refused to acknowledge such a thing—not about a member of the Rydianian royal family.

Prince Istvan might not have had anything to do with her father's dismissal from his lifelong service to the royal family or his subsequent banishment from the country, but that didn't mean Istvan wasn't one of them—raised to be like the uncaring, unfeeling royals who had destroyed her family.

"Does it take you long to do a sketch?" His smooth, rich voice interrupted her thoughts.

"No."

"How long does it usually take?"

She wasn't sure what to make of him going out of his way to make small talk. "Five to ten minutes. It all depends on how much detail work I do."

"That's amazing. It would take me twice as long to draw a stick figure." He sent her a friendly smile that made his baby blues twinkle.

She ignored the way her stomach dipped as she returned her focus to the drawing. Why did he have to be the prince from Rydiania? Why couldn't he just be a random guest at the resort?

She smothered a sigh and focused on her work. She took pleasure in the fact that she didn't have to do a true sketch of the prince. Her job was to exaggerate certain characteristics. She chose to elongate his chin and emphasize his perfectly straight white front teeth. His hair was perfectly styled, as though not a strand would dare defy the prince. She would fix that by drawing his hair a bit longer and messier. And then she took some creative liberty and added a crown that was falling off to the side of his head. A little smile pulled at the corner of her lips. It definitely wasn't the image of a proper prince.

The man on the page was more approachable. He didn't take himself too seriously. And this prince wouldn't endorse the demise of innocent and loyal subjects. If only fiction was reality.

With the outline complete, she started to fill in the sketch with a bit of color. When she first took this job at the resort, she'd considered just doing black-and-white sketches, but she was partial to colors. And it didn't take her much more time.

When she focused on the prince's blue eyes, she had a problem combining the blues to get that intense color. Maybe she should have just done a plain light blue color like she would have done for any other person. But it was though his eyes held a challenge for her. How could she resist?

When she glanced at him, it was though he could see straight through her. She wondered what he thought when he looked at her. But then again, he was a royal, so he probably didn't even see her—not really. He most likely saw nothing more than someone who was there to serve him.

Indigo switched up color after color. Her hand moved rapidly over the paper. He became distracted with his phone. With his attention elsewhere, it was easier for her to finish her task.

"I see you've decided to get a caricature done," a female voice said.

Indigo paused to glance over her shoulder to

find her boss approaching them. Hermione wore a warm smile. Indigo wondered if Hermione had a secret crush on the prince. It wouldn't be hard to imagine her with him.

But then again, Hermione was now sporting a large, sparkly diamond ring. And her fiancé was almost as handsome as the prince. Hermione and the prince made chitchat while Indigo continued to add more details to the sketch. At one point, she leaned back to take in the partial image. Her discerning gaze swept down over the page. She surprised herself. There wasn't one negative aspect of the sketch. How could that be?

No imperfection that had been exaggerated. No big front teeth sticking out. No bulbous nose. No pointy chin. Nothing but his hotness exaggerated on the page into a cute caricature. And the crown she'd added to make him look like a carefree prince—well, even that didn't look like a negative. In fact, it just upped his cute factor.

As Hermione moved on, Indigo was still puzzling over the image that lacked any of her normal exaggerations. Was this really how she saw him? Like some fun, easygoing and kind royal?

Obviously not. He was heir to the throne. He would do things just as they had been done before—stepping on loved ones and family for the good of the crown.

CHAPTER TWO

DID HE HAVE better things to do with his time? Yes.

Did he really care about the mounting messages on his phone? No.

Prince Istvan lifted his head and stared at the top of the young woman's head as she worked behind the easel. He shifted to the side to get a better view of her. Her long hair was pulled back into a ponytail that fell over her shoulder. His fingers tingled with the urge to comb their way through the dark, silky strands.

His gaze strayed to her gold name tag. Indigo. Such a pretty name for someone so strikingly beautiful.

His attention returned to her face. Lines formed between her fine brows as she concentrated on her work. A pert little nose led to heart-shaped lips that were just begging to be kissed. It was such a tempting idea.

Just then she glanced up. Their gazes caught and held, causing a warm sensation in his chest. Did she know he had been fantasizing about pulling her into his embrace? Without a word, her attention returned to the easel.

There was something about her that made him feel like they somehow knew each other, but as he searched his memory, he was certain if their paths had crossed he would have remembered her. She had an unforgettable natural beauty about her, from her big brown eyes with flecks of gold that made them twinkle to her pert nose and lush lips that tempted and teased.

But he didn't have time to be distracted. He had problems awaiting him back home. His father was reaching a point where his health was forcing him to step down from the throne. Istvan was expected to take on more and more royal duties in preparation for the transfer of power.

The problem was, the more responsibilities he took on, the more unhappy he became. It wasn't the work he didn't like—it was the lack of time he had to devote to his pet projects. He had taken under his wing the Arts for Children, Homes for All and his biggest project, We Care—a foundation to support sick children and their families. All such worthy causes, and all needed more attention than he could possibly give each of them once he ascended to the throne.

But with his name attached to the charities, more people stepped up to help. More people were willing to give of their time, energy and money. If he were to walk away now, the future of the foundations would be in jeopardy because they weren't designated as royal charities. To fall under the royal designation, each charity had to meet stringent criteria—including being established for a minimum of fifty years. His projects were still in their infancy. And quite honestly, he didn't want to walk away. It was good work—important work. The foundations put him in direct contact with the people of the kingdom in a way he never would have been if he'd secluded himself in the palace. How was he supposed to rule over people when he didn't know what was important to them?

He was quickly coming to the realization that his family was becoming antiquated. It was a sobering thought he didn't dare share with anyone.

What was wrong with him? He should feel like he was on top of the world, but as the day of his crowning approached, the more he felt himself withdrawing from his family.

He couldn't help but wonder if this was how his uncle felt before he'd abdicated the throne—not that Istvan was planning to do the same thing. He'd been young when it happened, but he clearly recalled the turmoil it'd caused his family. There couldn't be a repeat.

His phone started to ring. He withdrew it from his pocket. The caller ID said it was his eldest sister, Gisella. He could already guess what was on his sister's mind—royal business. She might not be the heir to the throne, but that didn't keep her from assuming an important place in the family business.

He could only imagine she was calling to admonish him for missing some meeting. He always heard the disapproving tone in her voice when he was away from the palace.

It wasn't like this trip had been spontaneous. It had been on his calendar for a year. He had the speed boat race tomorrow. And he intended to win. He wasn't going to let anyone ruin these few days of relaxation. He'd be back at the palace soon enough.

And so he pressed the ignore button on his phone. Whatever it was, it could wait.

"If you have somewhere else to be, I can finish this without you." The sweet, melodic voice drew him from his thoughts.

Istvan blinked and stared at the artist. "Excuse me. What did you say?"

"That I can finish this drawing without you and have it delivered."

"That won't be necessary." He forced a smile, reassuring her that everything was all right.

She looked at him for a moment longer but didn't say anything. It was impossible to tell what she was thinking behind those big brown eyes.

A few minutes later, the young woman released the white paper from the clips on the board. She grasped the paper and approached him. "Here you go."

He took the paper from her. He didn't know what he expected. Under normal circumstances, an artist would be very reserved in their work since he was, after all, a prince. So he supposed he expected something similar from Indigo.

But when he held the sketch out in front of him, he realized she'd treated him just like she had her other clients. In fact, for a moment he didn't recognize himself. Instead of smiling, he was frowning in the sketch. Was that how she saw him?

But the seriousness of the frown was offset by a crown that was sliding down the side of his head as his eyes were upturned, trying to figure out what was going on. He noticed the details from his eyes and lashes to the pucker lines in his rather large bottom lip.

Had she really been that observant? She was able to translate his thoughts to paper. Because he'd been thinking of how unhappy he was with the restraints the crown would place upon his life. But a casual observer would never pick up on it. This woman was keenly observant.

"This is remarkable," he said.

Her fine brows momentarily lifted, as though she were truly surprised by his praise. "I'm glad you like it."

"I think it's amazing that you can do all this in

just a matter of minutes. I wish I could do something like this."

"Have you ever tried?"

He shook his head. "No. But I'm sure any attempt I'd make would be a disaster."

"You'll never know until you give it a try."

Art had never been an important part of his upbringing. His lessons had consisted of the basics in grammar and math, but the emphasis had been on history, specifically the history of Rydiania, government and civics. There was no room in his busy schedule for sports or arts.

He wondered what he'd missed by not exploring the arts. Was he an undiscovered grand pianist? He immediately dismissed the idea. There was nothing wrong with the piano, but he had never been curious about it or drawn to it.

Perhaps he would have been good at playing the guitar—maybe he would have been the lead guitar player in a rock band. He struggled not to smile as he imagined his parents' horrified expressions if he'd wanted to go in that direction.

Indigo pursed her lips as her brows drew together. "You find the suggestion funny?"

Oh, no. He hadn't hidden his thoughts as well as he'd thought. "No. It's not that. I was thinking of my parents' reaction if I told them I was giving up the throne to pursue something in the arts field."

"Oh." Her lush lips smoothed out, and her

brows parted. "I'm guessing they would absolutely hate the idea."

His brows rose. "You sound as though you know them."

She shook her head. "No. Not at all. I… I was just guessing about their response."

He nodded in understanding. Just then the head of his security detail stepped up and whispered in his ear. His sister was eager to reach him and not happy that he wasn't answering his phone.

Istvan cleared his throat. "I must go now. But I want to thank you for this…interesting drawing. I've never had one like it. How much do I owe you?"

Color bloomed in her cheeks. "Nothing. It's courtesy of the resort."

"But surely I can tip you."

She shook her head. "I am paid well."

"I see." He hesitated. This never happened to him. Most people asked many things of him. Some requests he could accomplish, but there were many other requests that were far beyond his power. But this beautiful woman wanted nothing from him. He was intrigued.

"Sir, we must go," his head of security reminded him.

Even here on his uncle's island, far removed from his kingdom, his life was still not his own. "Yes. I'm coming." He turned back to Indigo. "I must leave, but I just want to thank you for this drawing. It's truly unique."

Her cheeks pinkened. "You're welcome."

And with that he walked away. He was tempted to glance over his shoulder at the woman who treated him like any other human instead of the crown prince. Was she really that immune to his charms? Or was there something more? Some other reason she kept a wall up between them?

Buzz. Buzz.

He didn't have time to consider the answers to his mounting questions. Royal duty took precedence over everything. His jaw tightened as he reached for his phone.

He didn't have to check the caller ID to know who was at the other end of the phone call. Princess Gisella.

"Hello." He struggled to keep the irritation out of his voice.

"It's about time. I've been trying to reach you. You should have known it was important, because I do not like making phone calls."

"I was preoccupied." He knew she was expecting an apology for not jumping when she'd called, but he was tired of feeling like their roles were reversed—tired of Gisella always proving she was the most loyal to the crown. "What do you need?"

"You. Back here at once."

He restrained a sigh. This was not their first conversation about his whereabouts or her utter displeasure with him for visiting their uncle's island. "I'll return after the weekend. I have a race to participate in."

"You shouldn't be racing. It's dangerous. You can't take frivolous chances with your life. You're the crown prince. If something happened…"

"You'd step in and be an amazing queen."

"Don't say that. It's like tempting fate."

Laughter erupted from his throat. "Gisella, you do worry too much."

"Someone has to. You certainly don't."

"I'll be safe."

"Make sure you are. What about the visit from the Spanish delegation? The festival is this weekend, and you must make an appearance."

"I'm sure you can charm them."

Gisella sighed. "I can't always fill in for you. You are, after all, the crown prince."

"Maybe you should be. You enjoy all that pomp and circumstance."

"Istvan!" Gisella's voice took on a warning tone, telling him that he was going too far.

"Relax. I'm just giving you a hard time."

There was a strained pause. "See that you are here early. There's a cabinet meeting on Monday morning, and you are to attend with the king. And you have yet to sit for your portrait. It is needed not only for the palace, but it is also to be added to the currency."

And he had been dragging his feet. He didn't

know how he felt about his face being on Rydiania's currency. Sure, it was only one denomination, while his father appeared on the rest. But still, it felt as though it were sealing his fate—hemming him into a life exactly like his parents'. The thought of being locked up in the palace for the rest of his life made him feel claustrophobic.

He'd much rather stay here on this sunny island with its colorful, fruity drinks and the most alluring artist. It was far more appealing than being cooped up with the royal painter for hours.

Suddenly a thought came to him. Perhaps sitting for the portrait didn't have to be as miserable as he'd been imagining. Perhaps it could be pleasurable.

Indigo's image came to mind. He wondered if she had any experience with personal portraits. He didn't know the answer, but it was something he planned to look into as soon as possible.

CHAPTER THREE

His VIVID BLUE eyes haunted her.

Later that afternoon, Indigo clipped a fresh paper to the easel. She couldn't stop thinking of the prince. He was not what she'd been expecting. Not at all.

Somehow she'd imagined him as a spoiled brat. He was not that. She'd expected him to be totally full of himself. He hadn't been. And she'd expected him to take himself too seriously—to the point where he wouldn't have been able to appreciate the sketch she'd done of him. And yet he'd genuinely seemed to like the silly sketch. What did that mean?

It would be so much easier to dislike the prince if he had some obvious negative qualities. But right now she was struggling to find something legitimate to dislike about him—other than his lineage.

As she bent over to retrieve a fresh pen from her large tote, she heard someone approaching. "Have a seat. I'll be right with you."

They didn't say a word, but she sensed their presence. She straightened, clipped the paper to the board and then glanced around it. She struggled not to gape when she found the prince sitting on the stool. Again.

Heat swirled in her chest. "Your Highness, you're back."

She noticed this time he was wearing a white T-shirt with the race logo on it. She felt an instant pang of disappointment at not getting another glimpse of his muscled chest. She swallowed hard.

When her gaze rose to meet his, she asked, "What can I do for you?"

"I would like to have another sketch done. I'm more than willing to compensate you."

"Another?" No one ever came back to her and requested a second sketch. "Did something happen to the first one?"

"No. Actually, I need another for a charity auction."

Charity? The prince? Really?

Nothing about the man sitting in front of her was like her father had warned her about the royal family. Istvan was not cold. He was not harsh. And he was not mean.

What was she supposed to make of this prince with his generous heart and dazzling smile that made her stomach dip? The only thing she knew was that the more time she spent with him, the more confused she became. It was best to keep her distance.

"Can't you use the sketch I already drew for you?"

"It can't be that one."

"Why? Was it too silly?" She'd been waiting for him to show his true colors.

He shook his head. "No. It was perfect. That's why I'm keeping it. I need another one for the auction."

"Something more serious?"

"Not at all. I enjoy your sense of humor. So have at it. I don't want any special treatment. You can do the same thing or something different. I don't care."

She inwardly groaned. What was it with this guy? He was making it impossible for her to dislike him. In fact, if she spent more time with him, she might fall for his azure-blue eyes and his sexy accent.

It was best to get this over with as quickly as possible. Indigo was certain that once she completed the sketch she wouldn't see the prince again.

In truth, she didn't need him to sit for her again. She had every detail of his handsome face memorized. She groaned inwardly.

The artist in her demanded she do something different than the first sketch. She never did duplicates of anything. Life was too short for repeats.

This time she decided to portray the prince in his royal world. She told herself it would be fun, but there was another reason—she needed a visual reminder that this man wasn't just another handsome face.

Her father had been obsessed with the royal family toward the end of his life. At the time, she couldn't understand why he went on and on about them. But as she grew older, she realized her father had considered his position as the king's secretary as much more than an occupation. To him, it was his life's calling—the position that had been handed down to him through the generations of his family's service to the royal family.

Not only had he been stripped of his calling, but he was then kicked out of the country like a traitor. It broke something in her father—something time and even love couldn't fix.

Indigo shoved the troubling thoughts to the back of her mind. Instead she focused on her work. She looked at the prince as little as possible, trying to work from memory. But she found herself questioning her memory time and again. Because it just wasn't possible for someone to look as good as him, from his high cheekbones to his strong chin to his perfectly straight nose.

And then there were his eyes. Oh, those eyes! She felt as though she were being drawn in every time their gazes connected. This time the prince wasn't distracted by his phone. This time his attention was solely on her. His unwavering gaze sent a current of awareness zipping through her veins.

She struggled to keep her hand from tremoring. That had never been a problem for her in the past. Why was she letting him get to her? He was just another guy. *Yeah, right.* He was anything but just another guy. And her traitorous body was well aware of it.

Her brush pen moved rapidly over the page. She forced herself not to go too fast. After all, this was her art, and it deserved to be her best.

When at last she finished, she removed the page from the easel and handed it over. She wasn't sure what he'd think of her image. This sketch had him wearing a serious expression with his exaggerated chin slightly upturned as he wore his crooked crown and a royal cape, while holding a scepter in his hand.

He was quiet for a moment as he took in the image. "Is that how you really see me? Looking down on the world?"

He didn't sound pleased. It seemed her image had struck a nerve. She wasn't sure if it was a good thing—that he cared how the world saw him—or a bad thing, because he had the power to get her fired. She hadn't considered that dire consequence when she'd indulged her imagination.

It was best she try and smooth things out. She swallowed hard. "It's not how I see you. I don't even know you. I was just having some fun. If you give it back, I'll try again."

He stood, quietly staring at the image. "No. I will keep it."

"But if you don't like it—"

"Your art has a way of making one look at themselves in a totally different light." At last he smiled. "I like it." He paused and stared at the sketch a little longer. "I really like it."

"Are you sure?" It was in her best interest to make the prince happy, even if it was the last thing she wanted to do. She could imagine her father scolding her for placating the heir to the throne.

"I am positive. I will find a special spot for this."

Perhaps in the wastebasket? She kept the thought to herself. She'd already pushed her luck as far as she imagined it would go that day.

His gaze lifted and met hers. "Is this the only thing you do?"

"Excuse me?"

"Do you do other forms of artwork besides the sketches?"

She nodded. "I do. This is just a side job that I've picked up."

"You have more than one job?" He looked impressed.

"You have no idea."

In addition to her work at the resort, she was constantly adding to her collection of portraits.

In her neighborhood, many of the residents were willing to pose for her. She was busy preparing for her first-ever gallery showing in Athens. It was a huge milestone. Plus, she helped care for her mother.

"I'd love to see some of your other work. Would that be possible? Do you have a website or something?"

She shook her head. "No website." But then she realized she'd taken a few photos of her latest pieces to show her agent. She pulled out her phone and pulled up the photos. "These are some recent pieces."

She wasn't sure why she was sharing any of this with him. It wasn't like they were friends— far from it. But it wasn't often she met someone who was interested in her work. And it felt good to be able to share it with him.

Her pieces were done in modern realism. There were paintings of her neighbors' daughters as they played, an older gentleman she'd met at the park and one of her mother. She painted what she saw and then gave the images her own interpretation.

Istvan paused on each photo. He was quiet as he studied them. She couldn't help but wonder what he was thinking. She wanted to ask, but she didn't dare. What if he hated them? As much as she tried to wear a tough outer shell, criticism still had a way of working past her well-laid defenses and planting a seed of doubt about her abilities.

But there was no way she was going to let him think his opinion mattered to her. Nothing could be further from the truth. She knew she was good at what she did. It wasn't her being conceited. It's what she'd been told by her agent, by clients and gallery owners. They were the people in the know.

She shifted her weight from one foot to the other. What was taking him so long? There were three photos for him to see. Unless he'd moved beyond those photos. Her chest tightened. Was he looking at her personal photos?

She moved slightly and craned her neck to get a glimpse of her phone. He was staring intently at the painting of her mother. Did he recognize her?

Indigo immediately scolded herself for over-thinking things. There was no way he would recognize her. Her family had moved away from Rydiania when she was very little, so he couldn't have been much older. If he didn't recognize her mother, what was it about the painting that held his attention?

She glanced off to the side and noticed a rather lengthy line of customers had formed. She'd never had this much interest in her sketches since she'd arrived on the island. And then she realized what all the attention was about—the prince.

It was time to draw this conversation to an

end. She cleared her throat. "Is there something else you need?"

He held her phone out to her. "These are good. No, they're great. You're very talented. So, then, why are you here doing caricatures?"

Because she needed the extra money to secure her mother a spot at the assisted living facility. But she wasn't about to reveal her struggles to the prince, who had no idea what it was to struggle for the things he wanted or needed.

"Work is work," she said.

He nodded as though he understood. "Thank you for sharing these with me. I see amazing things in your future." He turned as though to walk away, but then he turned back to her. "I was wondering if you'll be watching the race."

His inquiry caught her off guard. Why would he be interested in whether she'd be attending or not? Was he merely trying to make casual conversation? Or was it something more?

Was he flirting with her?

Laughter bubbled up inside her. She quickly stifled it. There was no way this handsome, eligible prince would be interested in her. Not a chance.

"I won't be able to attend. I have to work." She gestured to all the people lined up. The line kept growing. She really would have to work all day to get that many sketches completed.

"Surely they'll give you some time off to watch

the race, since most every guest at the resort will probably be in attendance."

What she heard him say was that, being the prince, he was the center of the universe, so everyone would want to see what he was doing. Her back teeth ground together. It took all her willpower to subdue her frustration with him. "I'm sorry. I really do have to work."

"I know your boss—the new owners of the resort. I could get you some time off." There was a gleam in his eyes. Was it a hopeful look?

She shook her head. "I need to get back to work."

It was only then that she noticed him turning his head and taking in the view of the long line, waiting to have their sketches done. "I understand."

And yet he continued to stand there. Why was he being so obstinate? Had he never been turned down before? And then it came to her that no one would turn him down. Well, that was, no one except her.

Secretly, she was tempted to learn more about this prince. If she had met Istvan under different circumstances—if she hadn't known his true identity—she would have liked him. And that right there worried her. She couldn't fall for the enemy, because her father had trusted the royal family and look where that had gotten him—dead in what should have been the prime of his life.

* * *

He should go.

And yet his feet didn't move.

Istvan was utterly intrigued by Indigo. The more time he spent with her, the more he realized she was unlike any other woman he had ever known. And he had known quite a few during his globetrotting years.

There were times when Indigo looked at him and he thought she might be interested in him. And then there were other times when their gazes met and he could see the hostility lurking in their depths. How could she dislike him? She didn't know him yet. Or was it that she held his lineage against him? She wouldn't be the first person.

Whatever it was that was going on behind her beautiful eyes, he wanted to know the answers. He wanted to walk with her on the beach, and as the water washed over their bare feet, he wanted to learn what made her tick. And then he wanted to talk some more.

Okay, maybe he wanted to do more than talk. His gaze lowered. After all, her lush lips had beckoned to him more than once. *Oh, yes.* He definitely wanted to explore them and see if her kisses were as sweet as the berries he'd had for breakfast that morning.

It wasn't that he lacked for female companionship, but none could compare to Indigo, who insisted on speaking to him as she did everyone else. That was it. He never did like being treated specially—making him stand out from the others. He didn't feel special. Not at all.

And maybe part of that had to do with his uncle. When Georgios had abdicated the throne, it had had a huge impact on Istvan. He didn't want to think about that now. It always put him in a foul mood.

He shoved aside the troubling thoughts as his gaze met hers once more. He had something much more pleasant in mind. He planned to ask Indigo to dinner.

Buzz. Buzz.

He wanted to ignore the phone, but as it continued to vibrate in his pocket, it was impossible to ignore. He knew he wasn't going to like it, whoever it was. He'd bet his crown that it was the palace with some other task that required his attention.

"You should get that," she said, as though relieved to have an excuse to brush him off.

A dinner invitation teetered on the tip of his tongue. But he had a feeling if he were to ask her to dinner right now, she would turn him down, and he didn't want that to happen. Maybe another time would be better—a time when there wasn't a line of people waiting for her attention.

He withdrew his phone and saw that it was indeed the palace. He pressed Decline. But when he glanced up and saw the irritation radiating from Indigo's eyes, he realized it was time for him to move on.

"I'll get out of your way." His gaze lingered on her beautiful face for a moment longer than necessary. And then with reluctance, he walked away.

Buzz. Buzz.

When he checked his phone's caller ID, he found it was the palace…again. Whatever they wanted must be important.

With a resigned sign, he pressed the phone to his ear. "Prince Istvan."

"This is the queen's secretary," the older woman said in a measured tone. "The queen would like to remind you that this weekend we are hosting a formal dinner for Spain's dignitaries."

And yet another reminder of the responsibilities awaiting him at home. But this royal regatta was his responsibility, too. It was being held in memory of his uncle. And since he seemed to be the only family member who wanted to remember his uncle, there wasn't a chance he was leaving Ludus Island before the festivities were concluded.

"You may tell the queen that I'll be unavailable this weekend."

"Yes, Your Highness. And the queen would like to remind you that Monday afternoon you have an appointment to sit for your portrait."

The thought of sitting there for the royal artist, who didn't know how to smile, much less make light conversation, sounded like a punishment Istvan hadn't earned. He didn't see why the man couldn't work from a photo. But Istvan had been informed that a photo just wouldn't do.

Who would want to sit in an uncomfortable chair for hours while their mind went numb from boredom? But he hadn't felt that way when he'd sat for Indigo to sketch him. Now, granted the caricature didn't take nearly as long, but she intrigued him. And he had a feeling she could carry her end of a conversation if they'd had a bit more time together.

Suddenly his whimsical thought of commissioning Indigo to do his portrait was taking on more substance, especially after viewing some of her formal work. He wondered if she would be up for a trip. He would definitely make it worth her time.

"Tell my mother I'll make time for the portrait, but I plan to do it on my terms."

"Your Highness?" There was a note of a question to the secretary's tone.

Istvan chose to ignore her inquiry. "I must go." And with that the call was concluded.

He had been butting heads with his parents for years now. They wanted things done their way—the way they'd always been done. He wanted change. He wanted the monarchy to act with compassion.

Once his father had let it slip that Istvan was just like his uncle—thinking the dynasty should change according to the people's whims. But as soon as the king said it, he'd retracted the words. He told Istvan that he would never be like Georgios—he would never walk away from his responsibilities—because he'd raised him different. He'd raised him to be a true king.

CHAPTER FOUR

AT LAST, HER shift was over.

Indigo stifled a yawn. Thanks to the prince's insistence on a second sketch, she'd had an endless line of excited subjects. And they'd all had questions about Istvan—questions Indigo did her best to discourage.

She flexed her fingers. Her entire hand ached. She repeatedly stretched her fingers wide apart, trying to ease the ache in them. It only helped to a certain extent. If she had known her sketches were going to be in such great demand, she might have negotiated for a per-sketch fee on top of her base pay.

She folded the easel, grabbed her supply caddy and started toward the resort. With evening closing in, the beach area had quieted down. Everyone must be inside getting cleaned up for dinner. Indigo's stomach rumbled at the thought of food. She hadn't had time for lunch today. She couldn't keep up this pace. If it continued, she might have to mention to Hermione about hiring another artist.

"Indigo." Hermione, the resort's manager, waved as she rushed to catch up with her. "How did the day go?"

Indigo wasn't sure how honest to be with her boss about the overwhelming line of people. On the other hand, it was job security. "There were people lined up all day."

Hermione smiled. "I've been hearing lots of good things about your work. We'll have to discuss extending your time at the resort."

"Thank you." Indigo wasn't sure how that would work out going forward. She had a lot of hopes and dreams relying on her upcoming gallery show. Still, it was like her father used to tell her—*don't take for granted what is in hopes of what may be.* "That sounds good."

"So the prince has taken a liking to your work." Hermione sent her a reassuring smile. "That is huge praise. He's very particular about what he likes."

Indigo should be pleased with this compliment, but it just made her feel more uncomfortable. And she didn't want her new friend to think she was tripping over herself for the prince. "I... I didn't do anything for him that I haven't done for the other guests."

"And that's what makes it even more special." *Ding.*

Hermione pulled her phone from her pocket.

She read the message on the screen and then sighed.

Indigo hoped it wasn't bad news. Hermione had been kind to her. Indigo liked to think they were becoming fast friends. She appreciated how Hermione had taken a chance on hiring her when neither of them had known if the idea of caricatures would be a hit or a miss with the resort guests. Lucky for Indigo, her fun sketches had been met with great enthusiasm. And now she wished she could think of a way to pay Hermione back for believing in her.

"Is there something I can help with?" Indigo asked.

Hermione glanced up from her phone. Her fine brows were drawn together as though she were in deep thought. "Um…no. Thanks. I've got it."

Indigo didn't believe her. "I'd like to help if I can. After all, my shift is over."

Hermione sent her a hesitant look. "If you're sure." When Indigo nodded, Hermione said, "I wouldn't ask, but there's a snafu with a shipment at the dock, and on my way out of the building, I forgot to drop off some papers at the gallery."

"Okay. Let me take the paperwork to the gallery. It's on my way out."

Hermione withdrew a clipped stack of papers from her black leather portfolio. "Here you go. Everything is there that they'll need for the shipment." She then gave Indigo specific instructions on where to take the papers and whom to hand them to. It all seemed very straightforward and easy enough to handle.

"You're getting rid of an exhibit?" Indigo had been to the gallery many times. She loved to admire the various artworks. She hoped someday to have one of her paintings displayed in such a prestigious gallery.

Hermione shook her head. "We have agreements with other galleries. We exchange various pieces. This time we're loaning out *Clash of Hearts*."

Indigo remembered the piece because of its vibrant colors from hot pink to silver. It had been created of conjoined hearts of varying sizes that were repeated over the entire canvas. "It's a beautiful piece."

"Thank you. I was the one to acquire it." Hermione smiled brightly. When her phone dinged again, she said, "I better get going. Are you sure you don't mind doing this?"

"Not at all. I'll see you tomorrow." She gave a little wave before turning toward the resort.

Once inside the resort, the plush carpeting in the wide hallways smothered the sound of her footsteps. The resort was quiet. It was a lot like walking through a museum with its many art pieces, not only in the gallery but also displayed on the many hallways.

She found herself referring to it as a common-

er's palace. But then again, why shouldn't the resort be fashioned after a palace, since its founder
was once a king—a king who stepped aside to let
his brother take over. In the process, King Georgios not only gave up his crown but he also lost
his country and his family.

And though the Ludus Resort had every ame-
nity imaginable and looked magnificent, it still
wasn't a home. Both the former king and Indigo's
father had died without ever being able to reclaim
what they had loved and lost—their homeland.
And for that she felt so sorry for both of them.

She approached the entrance of the Ludus Gallery. The large glass door silently swung open
without much effort. The gallery was divided between the large front section with its tall white
walls that gave the space a wide-open, airy feel
and the back section that was the opposite, with
black walls and spotlights used to highlight the
gallery's headliner.

In this case, it was the Ruby Heart that was the
shining star. Indigo had seen it once before, but
it had been in passing because the gallery had
been so busy. But today the gallery was quiet. It
would give her a chance to admire the precious
stone for as long as she wanted.

She approached the glass case. The stone was
quite large. It was much too big to ever be worn as
a piece of jewelry. The many cuts looked to have
been very carefully planned, and each picked up

the light, making it sparkle as though it were actually alive and full of energy.

She noticed a sign that displayed background information about the stone. Just as she was about to lean in closer to read the words, she heard someone behind her.

"It's beautiful," the smooth, deep voice said.

Indigo didn't have to turn around to know who was behind her—Prince Istvan. Not sure what to do, she continued to stare at the magnificent jewel. "Yes, it is."

"And yet it pales in beauty compared to you." His voice was so soft that it was as if the words had caressed her.

Heat gathered in her chest before rushing up her neck and setting her cheeks ablaze. Thank goodness she wasn't facing him.

She swallowed hard. And then hoped when she spoke her voice didn't betray her. "I've never seen a gem so large."

He moved next to her. "Did you read the legend attached to it?"

Her heart pounded. Her mouth grew dry. "Um, no. I was just about to do that."

"Let me." He leaned toward her as he focused on the display. "'The legend of the Ruby Heart. If destined lovers gaze upon the Ruby Heart at the same time, their lives will be forever entwined.'"

Lovers? Suddenly a very hot and enticing image of her and Istvan entwined in each other's arms filled her mind. She gave herself a mental shake, chasing away the temptation. Why, oh, why had she stopped here? She should have just dropped off the papers and left. Then she could have avoided this awkward moment.

"Hmm…" The sound rumbled in his throat for a moment, almost as though he were a Cheshire cat eyeing up his prey—in this case, that would be her. "I wonder if they might be referring to us."

It felt as though the air-conditioning had been turned off and a blowtorch had been lit in her face. Her mouth went even drier as she struggled to swallow. "I'm quite certain they are mistaken in this case." How she got those words out and did not melt into a puddle on the floor was utterly beyond her. "I should be going."

The only problem was that he was standing between her and the hallway she needed to access to reach the business office, where she was to drop off the papers.

"Having second thoughts?" he asked.

When she glanced at him, she saw the amusement dancing in his eyes. "Not at all. You just happen to be standing in my way."

With an amused smile plastered on his undeniably handsome face, he stepped out of the way. "I look forward to our next meeting."

His words made her heart flutter. She tried to tell herself that it was just casual flirtation, but there was this look in his eyes. Other men had looked at her that way, so she recognized it. It was a look of attraction—a look that said he was interested in taking their relationship to the next level. Her heart went *thump-thump* in her chest.

The prince is interested in me?

She moved quickly toward the privacy of the little hallway. The distance from the prince didn't stop the heat from gathering in her chest and rushing to her face. She resisted the urge to fan herself.

She came to a stop in front of an open door. The sign on the door read Museum Curator. This was the right place. She rapped her knuckles on the doorjamb.

"Come in."

She stepped inside and noticed a messy desk off to the side. A middle-aged man with reading glasses perched on the end of his nose glanced up from a computer monitor. "Can I help you?"

"Yes. Hermione asked me to drop these off." She held out the clipped papers.

"Oh, yes. I was waiting for them." He accepted the papers. "Thank you."

"You're welcome."

It was time to leave, but she hesitated. Was the prince still in the gallery waiting for her? The thought sent her heart racing. She told herself it was the anxiety of dealing with his incorrigible flirting again. Nothing more.

"Was there something else?" the man asked.

"Um…" She quickly weighed her options. "Is there another exit?"

The man arched a brow in puzzlement. "There's the back exit. In the hallway, go to the right. And then make another right. It will take you to the loading area."

"Thank you."

She just wasn't ready to face the prince again. Not yet. She turned right just as the man had instructed.

Her steps were quick as she moved through the hallway. When her hands touched the metal door handle, she pushed it open. She breathed a sigh of relief. She'd escaped. But escaped what?

She wasn't prepared to answer that question. She shouldn't have let Istvan get to her. If she let her guard down with the handsome prince, it would lead to nothing but more heartache. She'd already had enough of that to last her an entire lifetime.

CHAPTER FIVE

THE GRAND RACE was about to begin.

It was the following afternoon, and Indigo couldn't deny that she was a bit curious about the regatta. She'd never been to a boat race before. And just as the prince had predicted, her line of guests had dissipated as the magical hour neared. Even Adara, the resort's concierge, had stopped by to let her know it would be all right for her to take in the race.

What would it hurt? After all, it wasn't like she was going there with the intent to see the prince. She was going because it was the biggest event on the island and everyone was going to watch the boat race, leaving her nothing else to do.

With her art supplies secured in a locker at the resort, she made her way to the area of the beach where the race was to start. However, she stood at the back of a sea of people. There was no way she'd make it to the front. And from back here she wouldn't be able to see a thing.

She glanced around, looking for a better vantage point. Just south of where she stood were cliffs. She didn't know if she could make it up there, but she'd give it a try. And so she started walking at a rapid pace.

When she found a trail that appeared to lead to higher ground, she followed it. It was a bit rugged and steep at times. Her sandals were not ideal for this trek, but that didn't deter her. And when the trail finally leveled off, she noticed a small clearing, and in the distance was a cliff.

She wasn't the only one to have this idea. Other people were gathered there. Some of the people she recognized as employees of the resort. She wondered if they were supposed to be working, like her. Still, if there were no people at the resort needing anything, why not indulge?

She made it to an open spot along the stone wall. At last, she could see the boats. In fact, they weren't that far away. And Prince Istvan's boat was easy to spot, with its host of flags. The top flag was a deep purple with a gold crown, signaling that there was a member of the royal family aboard.

A loud horn blew. Was this to signal the start of the race? Indigo was curious to see if Istvan would win. His boat was the same length as the others. She wondered if there were limitations on the boat size.

The boats started their engines and then moved into position. Since there were too many to line up in a single line, she assumed each boat had some sort of tracking device to keep track of its time.

And then she spotted Istvan standing behind the wheel of his boat. He was shirtless—again. If she were to paint him—not that she had any plans of doing such a thing—she'd be inclined to include his impressive chest and those six-pack abs. She subdued a laugh when she thought of the horrid looks such a painting would receive from the royal family.

As she continued to stare down at Istvan, he turned. His gaze scanned the crowd, and then it was as though he'd singled her out. His gaze paused. And then he waved. Surely he couldn't be waving at her. As everyone around her raised their hand to wave back, she resisted. It was a small resistance, but she had to prove—even if only to herself—that she was strong enough to resist his charms.

The horn blew again. The prince took his seat. Her gaze strayed across a digital clock at the end of the dock. Red numbers counted down from ten. And then with a third and final blow of the horn, the boats took off with a roar and a spray of water.

She watched as the prince guided his boat into the lead. Something told her it was where Istvan was most comfortable. And then the boats moved out of sight. From what she'd heard from the people she'd sketched, the race encircled the island. And until they returned, there was nothing here to see.

She followed the trail back down to the resort, where she nearly bumped into one of Prince Istvan's security detail. The man was quite tall. She had to crane her neck to look at his face. And then there were the dark sunglasses that kept his eyes hidden from the world.

"Sorry," she said. "I didn't see you there."

"Ms. Castellanos?"

"Yes." What did he want with her?

"This is for you." He handed her a small envelope before walking away.

She stared at the sealed envelope. It took her a moment to figure out what must be inside... the prince was insisting on paying her for the sketches, even after she'd told him it went against resort policy. Although the extra money would help her mother, she just couldn't keep it. She didn't want to lose her job at the resort.

But she was curious to see how much the prince valued her work. That couldn't be against the rules, right? She slipped her finger in the opening of the envelope and then carefully released the flap.

She reached inside and pulled out a folded slip of paper. This certainly wasn't a check. Disappointment assailed her. So if the prince wasn't attempting to pay her, what did he want?

She unfolded the paper and began to read.

Meet me at the Whale-of-a-Time Suite. 6 p.m.

That was it?

She turned the paper over to see if he'd written more. He hadn't. What in the world was this about? Was this his attempt to ask her to dinner—or something more intimate? Either way, it wasn't working for her. Besides if he knew who she was, he wouldn't want anything to do with her. And then she realized what she intended to do—stand up a prince. Who did such a thing?

The answer was easy…someone who knew the truth about the royal family of Rydiania. They were cold and ruthless. How many times had her father told her so while he drowned his sorrows in scotch?

And so on her way back to retrieve her art supplies, she passed a wastebasket. She paused. Was she really going to do this?

And then she heard the echo of her father's words: *Don't trust a royal.*

I won't, Dad. I remember.

She dropped the note into the trash and kept going. Prince Istvan would soon realize that he couldn't have everything he desired—and that included having her.

He sat alone.

Istvan checked the time. Again.

She was late. He had no patience for tardiness. It had been drilled into him since he was a young boy that you should be early for occasions. Apparently Indigo didn't believe in that bit of logic. As of that moment, she was thirteen and a half minutes late.

This did not bode well for hiring her to do his formal portrait. The painting had to be completed on a specific deadline as stipulated in the contract he'd had drawn up. The Treasury Department ran by a strict timeline. If he were smart, he'd give up on the idea of having Indigo paint his portrait.

Still, he hesitated. Maybe something had had happened to her. Maybe she had been unavoidably detained. The thought that something might have happened to her bothered him.

He signaled for Elek, his most trusted guard. When the man approached him, Istvan asked, "Did you personally hand Indigo the note?"

The man clasped his hands together as he leaned down. "Yes, Your Highness."

"And did she read it?"

"I do not know, sir. I was called away before she had a chance to open the envelope."

"Well, something must have happened or she would be here." He stood, sending the chair legs scraping over the floor. He was no longer Interested in eating. "We must check on her."

"Your Highness?" Elek looked confused.

"We'll go to her room. Find out what room she's in."

"Yes, sir." Elek pulled out his phone and placed a call.

Istvan began to pace. Something must be terribly wrong or she'd be here. The thought of anything happening to the pretty artist bothered him more than he was expecting.

Elek returned. "She's not staying at the resort."

Istvan sighed. "Of course she's not. She's an employee. I should have thought of that. Do you have her home address?"

Elek nodded. "They didn't want to give it to me, so I had to mention your name."

"It's fine." He would do what it took to make sure Indigo was all right. "Let's go."

Elek didn't immediately move.

"What?" Istvan was anxious to get to the bottom of what had delayed Indigo.

"Are you sure about this?" Elek didn't speak up unless he felt it was in the prince's best interest. "You could try calling her instead."

"Did you get her number?" When Elek nodded, Istvan said, "Well, let's have it."

He reached for his phone and quickly dialed the number. It rang and rang. And then it switched to voice mail.

"Hi. I can't answer the phone right now. I'm probably working on my next masterpiece. Just leave your name, number and a brief message, and I'll get back to you as soon as I can." *Beep.*

Istvan disconnected the call. He wasn't interested in leaving a message. He wanted to know why she'd stood him up. The thought pricked his ego. He'd never been stood up. There had to be a serious reason. And he wasn't going to rest until he knew what it was.

Because the more he thought of Indigo—and he found himself thinking of her quite a lot lately—the more certain he was that he wanted to know more about her.

She didn't appear to be easy to win over. She certainly wasn't swayed by titles. And that's what he admired about her.

If she were to paint his portrait, she would breathe some freshness into his image, just as he wanted to breathe freshness into the monarchy. He recalled the long talks he'd had with Uncle Georgios about the state of the monarchy. Though they didn't agree on everything, there was one area where they both were in agreement—the monarchy needed to change.

And Indigo was his first step in showing the world that when it was his turn to step up to the throne, he would do things differently. So he had to find out what was keeping her.

CHAPTER SIX

SHE COULDN'T STOP thinking of him.

Why would a prince ask her to dinner?

Indigo had absolutely no answer for that—at least none that she was willing to accept. Because there was no way someone like him would be interested in someone like her. No way at all.

And if he thought they were going to have a quick island romp before he flew off to his palace, he could think again. Even if his family hadn't destroyed hers, she was never one for a quick fling. It just wasn't her thing.

"Indi, do you know where I left my book?" her mother called out from the living room.

"Give me a second and I'll look for it."

Indigo had arrived home from work a little while ago. She'd grabbed a shower and switched into a summer dress. Her little two-bedroom apartment didn't have air-conditioning, and the dress was light and airy.

This summer was unusually hot. The first thing she'd done upon arriving home was to open all the windows. The fan in the living room was already on for her mother.

Indigo glanced in the bedroom mirror. Her hair was still damp from her shower, but it wouldn't stay that way for long. She twisted the long strands and pinned them to the back of her head.

And then she headed for her mother's bedroom. Her mother had been reading a historical series about Scottish highlanders. Her mother read a lot of different things, from romances to cozy mysteries to biographies. Now that her mother's health was failing and she couldn't get around the way she wanted, she said she liked to escape the walls of their apartment through the words in a book.

Indigo glanced around her mother's small bedroom. There were stacks of books everywhere. Some new, a lot old and there were magazines added in. "What did you say the title was?"

Her mother called it out and then added that it should have been on the side of the bed. It was then that Indigo was able to spot it.

She carried it to the living room. "Here you go. Do you need anything else?"

"I don't think so. Why, are you going somewhere?"

"We need groceries." And there was no way she could unwind right now. Every time she closed her eyes, the image of the prince was there.

A walk might help. "Is there anything special you want?"

"I have a list on the counter. There's not much. Just a few things." Her mother frowned.

"What's wrong? Are you in pain?"

Her mother shook her head. "I'm fine." She smiled, but it didn't reach her eyes. "I just feel horrible that I've become such a burden to you."

"Mama, don't ever think like that. I love having you around." And she meant it. She would be lost without her mother in her life.

Her mother's eyes filled with unshed tears. "How did I get so lucky to have such a wonderful daughter?"

Indigo shook her head. "I'm not special."

"Of course you are. And as soon as I have a place to move where I can get by on my own, you'll be able to have your life back. You should be out dating, not staying home, looking after me."

"Mama, I love you. I know you want your independence back, but until that happens, I love having you here."

A tear splashed onto her mother's pale cheek. "I love you, too."

Indigo knew how important it was to her mother to live on her own once more. It's part of the reason she'd taken the job at the resort. Between that income and hopefully the money she would make at her very first gallery showing, she'd have enough money to get her mother into an assisted living center.

The problem was that this was her first gallery showing. She had absolutely no idea how well her paintings would sell. But she wouldn't give up. She'd do whatever it took to make sure her mother was happy.

Knock-knock.

She wondered who that could be. Perhaps her aunt was stopping by to visit. The sisters were really close. In fact, they were best friends.

"Are you expecting Aunt Aggie?"

"No. But you know she drops by whenever she gets a chance. And she did mention that she had a new book to loan me as soon as she finished reading it. Maybe she finished it sooner than she expected." Her mother's face lit up.

Indigo stepped into the small foyer and opened the door. For a moment, the world stood still. There, standing before her, was Prince Istvan. Her heart lodged in her throat. *What in the world?*

She blinked. She had to be seeing things. Her pulse raced. There was no way he was on her doorstep. But after she blinked twice, he was still standing before her.

"Indigo, we need to talk." His voice was deep, with a heavy accent.

"Indi, send your aunt in," her mother called from the other room.

Indigo didn't want her mother to see the prince

and get upset. So she closed the door in the prince's face. "It's not Aunt Aggie." She struggled to sound normal. "Just someone who knocked on the wrong door."

"I hope you helped them."

"I did." She reached for her purse. "Now I'm off. I'll be home a little later."

"Okay. I'm going to read some more."

When Indigo opened the door again, the prince's brows were drawn into a formidable line, while irritation showed in his eyes. Obviously he wasn't used to people closing the door in his face. But to be fair, she wasn't used to people tracking her down at home.

She raised her finger to her lips to silence him until the door was shut and they were a few steps away. Then she paused and turned to him. "How did you find me?"

He paused as though he hadn't been expecting that question. "I had someone ask at the resort for your address."

"And they just gave it to you?" She would have to speak with Hermione.

His lack of a response meant he was accustomed to getting any information he needed. She should have known. If you were royalty, the rules didn't apply to you.

She huffed and crossed her arms. "Why are you here?"

"I want to know why you missed dinner. Did you have an emergency?"

"No." Why would he think that? In the next breath, she realized he wasn't used to being turned down. "Now, I need to be going."

"We need to talk."

She shook her head. "If this is about dinner, I can't."

His dark brows rose high on his forehead. "It doesn't have to be dinner. I would just like a moment of your time."

She tilted her chin upward until their gazes met. "And if I say no, you'll just go away."

Frustration shimmered in his eyes. He wordlessly stared back at her, letting her know he wasn't going anywhere until he had his say.

Tired of the staring game, she said, "I'm going to the market. If you want to walk with me, you can have your say."

"You want me to go grocery shopping?" His voice held a surprised tone.

"It's up to you." She turned and began walking.

For a moment, she heard no footsteps behind her. Was it possible he'd finally given up? She ignored the sense of disappointment that came over her.

And then she mentally admonished herself for having any sort of feelings where the prince was concerned. Because even if he was drop-dead gorgeous and persistent, in the end, he was a royal. And even though she was a Rydianian by birth, she'd promised herself as a child that she would never claim her heritage as a Rydianian citizen. As an adult, she'd never traveled to her birthplace. She preferred to focus her energy on the here and now versus what had once been.

"Wait up." She heard rapid footsteps behind her.

She didn't slow down. What was so important to him? She couldn't deny that she was curious. But she wasn't curious enough to turn back.

He fell in step with her. "How far away is this market?"

"Afraid of a little exercise?"

"Not at all. But these shoes aren't the best for walking long distances."

She glanced down to see he wore a pair of sand-colored loafers. "You don't have to walk with me."

"I want to." He settled a ball cap on his head and obscured his eyes with dark sunglasses. "Listen I'm sorry for overstepping."

The fact he realized that even a prince could overstep impressed her, but she still wasn't ready to let down her guard with him. *Don't trust a royal.* Her father's words echoed in her mind. He'd repeated them countless times over the years. It left an indelible impression.

"The market is only a couple of blocks away." She wasn't sure if it was her attempt at making peace or her way of dissuading him from following her.

The thing about Prince Istvan that worried her the most was his way of confusing her. She knew she should see him as the enemy. And yet there was a part of her that was curious about Istvan. Why was he going out of his way to speak to her? It wasn't like she was rich or famous. And she certainly wasn't a royal descendant. In royal terms, that would make her a nobody. So what was his interest in her?

"Are you this hard on all the men who try to ask you to dinner?" The prince's voice interrupted her thoughts.

"Only the princes." She couldn't believe she'd made that little quip until the words passed her lips.

"I see. So if I was someone else, you would have consented to dinner?"

She turned her head so that their gazes would meet. "You can never be anyone but who you are—heir to the throne."

"Ouch. You make that sound akin to a deadly disease."

His choice of words made her think of her father. In his case being close to the royals had been exactly like a deadly disease that in the end took his life. It might not have been at their hands, but they couldn't deny the role they'd played in his untimely demise.

They continued walking in silence because she had nothing nice to say to him. When she thought of her father and how he'd been treated after a lifetime of duty and devotion, it made her furious.

When she reached her destination, she turned to him. "The walk is over."

She pulled open the door and stepped inside the small market that she knew like the back of her hand. She visited the Samaras Market numerous times a week because she liked to cook with fresh vegetables. Since her mother had been diagnosed with heart failure along with some other health conditions, Indigo had made it her mission to help her mother in every way she knew how, including a vegetarian diet filled with fruits and vegetables. In the end, they both felt better.

She grabbed a basket and moved toward the fresh produce to see what they'd gotten in that week. All the while, she could feel Istvan's gaze on her—following her. He certainly was persistent.

When she picked up some tomatoes, he said, "Those don't look ripe. You might want to try the ones up higher." He pointed to some other tomatoes. "They look like they'll be more flavorful."

She couldn't help but smile at the prince offering her shopping advice. "Istvan, do you really expect me to believe you do your own shopping?"

"Who's this Istvan, you speak of? My name's

Joe. And I shop here all the time." He grabbed some tomatoes and placed them in his own basket.

He had a basket? He was shopping, too? Her gaze jerked around to meet his. She couldn't believe he was working this hard to get her attention.

Perhaps it wouldn't hurt to play along for a little bit. "So, Joe, how do you feel about zucchini?"

He shrugged. "I'm neutral on the subject."

"I see. And how about olives? Do you prefer black or green?"

"Green, for sure."

She couldn't resist the smile that pulled at her lips. "Are you planning to follow me through the whole market?"

"Who, me?" His voice held an innocent tone. "I'm just here to do a little shopping."

She honestly didn't know what to make of him. One minute he was infuriating, with the way he took advantage of his royal status, and the next minute he was acting like he was a normal person who was just trying to create some sort of bridge between them.

Secretly she was swooning just a little. After all, what woman didn't want a prince tripping over himself to impress her? Not that she was going to let on to him that his actions were starting to work on her.

As they made their way through the market, making small talk about various items, she noticed the puzzled looks the other patrons were giving them. Maybe because he was wearing sunglasses inside. Between the glasses and the dark ball cap, it was harder to make out his identity.

Or maybe it was his security team that had given him way. But when she glanced back, she noticed his entourage was nowhere to be seen. Was it possible he'd told them to remain outside?

"Why are you doing this?" she asked.

"Just like you, I need a few things." He scanned the pasta before adding his selection to his almost-full basket.

"And what exactly are you going to do with all that food once you buy it?"

"Eat it, of course." His tone was serious as he moved onto some jarred sauce.

She rolled her eyes. Was he always so obstinate? She couldn't help but wonder what it'd be like to spend the evening with the prince. Not that she was planning to do it or anything else. But it didn't mean she couldn't wonder about these things.

He was certainly going through a lot of bother to speak with her. And the funny thing was he never said a word about what he had on his mind. As the minutes passed and their baskets grew full, her curiosity was getting the best of her.

But by then they were at the checkout with a fresh loaf of bread topping each of their baskets. The bread was still warm from the oven. As she inhaled the aroma, her mouth watered. They were definitely having it for dinner. Her mother loved fresh-baked bread dipped in seasoned olive oil.

He let her check out first. When the checker told her the total, Istvan said, "I've got it."

She frowned at him. "No, you don't."

He looked at the checker. "You can just add it to my order."

Her gaze swung around to the checker. "Don't you dare." Then she reached in her wallet and produced the appropriate amount of money. She held it out to the checker. "Here you go."

The young man shrugged his shoulders before taking the money. He quickly counted out her change. And then Indigo turned a challenging look to Istvan.

He was wearing a smile. "You are unlike anyone I've ever known."

She didn't think she was that unusual. "Because I like to pay for my own groceries?"

His gaze held hers. And when he spoke, his rich voice dropped down a tone. "No. Because you are fiercely independent, very stubborn and utterly enchanting."

Her stomach dipped. Why exactly was she resisting spending more time with him? In that moment, the answer totally eluded her.

CHAPTER SEVEN

THIS WAS BETTER than a dinner date.

Wait. Had that outrageous thought really crossed his mind?

Istvan gave himself a mental shake.

He had never been grocery shopping before, but if it was this entertaining every time, he wouldn't mind doing it more often. But something told him it wouldn't have been half as much fun without Indigo.

She was as stubborn as she was beautiful. And the more he was around her, the greater the challenge became to work his way past her cool exterior. He'd seen the way she'd looked at him at the beach, and he knew the attraction went both ways. But for whatever reason, she was fighting it.

Once he paid for his groceries and they stepped outside, he offered to carry her groceries. To his surprise, she let him. It was the first thing she'd let him do for her. It was to the point where he almost thanked her for letting him carry her groceries. Then he realized how ridiculous that sounded and instead said nothing.

"This has been an interesting trip to the market," she said. "But I must know what brought you to my door."

So she was curious. Good. That was a step in the right direction. He was pleased to know his banter had actually produced the results he wanted.

"I tried to call, but you didn't answer."

"That was you?" When he nodded, she said, "When it said the caller ID was blocked, I figured it was a spam call."

"Spam? I've been referred to a lot of ways. Some good, some not so good. But I've never been called that."

An awkward silence ensued before she asked, "And what was so important that you had to see me?"

"I have a proposal for you."

She glanced over at him. Suspicion blazed in her eyes. "Dare I ask what sort of proposal?"

"I think you'll like it."

"I won't know until you tell me."

He cleared his throat. Surely even she wouldn't turn down this proposition. Then again, he was finding that he wasn't able to predict Indigo's reactions. It's part of what he liked so much about her. "I would like to hire you."

Her fine brows rose. "Hire me to do what? Cook for you?"

"Hmm… Now that you mention it, that's not a bad idea. Maybe we'll have to negotiate that later." He sent her a teasing smile. "Right now, I'd like to commission you to do my formal portrait."

She stopped walking. She was quiet, as though she were digesting his words. "You want me to paint you?"

"Yes."

She stared at him like he'd suddenly sprouted a third eye. Then, in a calm voice, she said, "No."

She'd turned him down? Really? Suddenly his amusement over her stubbornness turned to agitation. Fun and games were fine for a bit, but this was serious business for him. Did she have any idea how many artists had vied for the honor of painting his formal portrait?

He had to try again. "Don't you realize this would make your career? You could name your price after this. You could take on any project."

"I do. And the answer is still no."

He knew Indigo was different and did things in her own way. The other thing he knew about her was that her art was very important to her. So then, why would she turn down this prime opportunity?

Perhaps he hadn't explained it well enough. "This portrait I'd like to hire you to do would be high-profile. It will be my official portrait. It will be used for postage stamps, currency and who knows what else."

"That's nice for you, but the answer is still no."

Was it his imagination or had her pace picked up? Was she trying to get away from him? But why? The more he was around her, the more the questions came to him. "Why are you so ready to turn down such a great opportunity?"

She stopped and turned to him. She leveled her shoulders and lifted her chin ever so slightly. "I know you aren't used to being told no, but I have other obligations."

"Move them." It wasn't until the words were out of his mouth that he realized how much he sounded like his father. And that wasn't a good thing.

"No." She glared at him.

This conversation had most definitely taken a wrong turn. He swallowed hard. "My apologies. That didn't come out right. I meant to say that if there's anything I can do to make this an option for you, all you have to do is say the word. I think your work is exceptional, and it has a freshness to it that I'm looking for."

A myriad of expressions filtered over her face. She could say more with her eyes than with her lips, which were currently pursed together.

As the strained silence lingered, he grew impatient. "Will you do it?"

"No." She resumed walking.

At this point he should turn and walk away. With anyone else, that's exactly what he would do, but there was something special about Indigo—*erm, about her work.*

He'd give it one last try and then he was done. If fame and worldwide recognition wouldn't do it, perhaps money would work. "I can pay you." And then he mentioned a large sum of money. "Imagine what you could do with that money."

Her steps slowed. She was still moving—still not saying anything—but he knew he had her attention. She stopped and turned to him. "You can't be serious."

"Of course I am."

She didn't say no this time. In fact, she didn't say anything as she resumed walking, presumably to give his offer serious consideration.

She suddenly stopped. Then slowly she turned to him. "Why me?"

"Because I like your style. It's original, and it has depth to it."

"I'm sure your family already has an artist chosen to do your portrait."

"Don't worry about my family. I'll take care of them." He was certain his mother would fight him about this, but in the end, he would win. After all, he was heir to the throne. His parents would have to get used to the idea that he didn't plan to do things the way they wanted them done. "So you'll take on the project?"

She hesitated. Her gaze moved down the sidewalk as though she were weighing her options. But what was there to consider? He didn't know anyone who would pass up this opportunity, not to mention the small fortune he was willing to pay.

They began walking again. He was starting to think there was more to Indigo's aversion to him than just playing hard to get, but how could that be? It wasn't like they'd ever met before. Maybe she had something against rich people. But if that was the case, she wouldn't work at the Ludus Resort. He was overthinking this. Maybe it was as simple as her being nervous around a crown prince. But she sure didn't act nervous—at least not since their first meeting.

Indigo was a puzzle, and he longed to figure out how all the pieces fit together. And this trip to his kingdom would provide him with that opportunity. So long as she agreed to go with him.

When they came to a stop in front of her apartment building, he asked, "What do you say?"

"I can't just take time off from my new job at the resort." She worried her bottom lip.

"Don't worry about the resort. I'll take care of it. Your job will be safe."

Her eyes momentarily widened. Then she said, "That's right. You're friends with Hermione." Her gaze studied his. "I'll need twenty-five percent up-front."

She wasn't afraid to negotiate for what she wanted. Good for her. "Done."

"And the remainder upon completion of the portrait."

"Done." Then he held his hand out to her. "Shall we shake on it?"

Her gaze moved to his hand. She hesitantly placed her hand in his. He immediately noticed the smoothness of her skin. As her fingertips slid over the sensitive skin of his palm, sparks of attraction flew between them. A current of anticipation zinged up his arm and set his heart pounding. Oh, yes, this was going to be the most amazing adventure.

She withdrew her hand far too quickly, breaking the connection. He instinctively rubbed his fingertips over his palm as the sensation of her touch faded away.

And then recalling the contract, he retrieved it from Elek and then held it out to Indigo. "Here's a formal agreement. Read it over, sign it and bring it with you. My car will pick you up first thing Monday. Six a.m. sharp."

She accepted the papers. "To take me where?"

"To my private jet. Don't worry. We won't start working Monday. You'll have time to settle into your suite of rooms at the palace."

"The palace?" Confusion showed in her eyes.

"You surely didn't think we'd be completing the portrait here, did you?"

"I, uh, hadn't considered that this would include travel." She frowned.

"If you haven't been to Rydiania, I can promise you that it's beautiful. And while you're at the palace, you'll have access to its amenities."

She shook her head. "I can't."

"Can't what?" Maybe it was him, but he was having a difficult time understanding her today. "Enjoy the amenities?"

"All of it. I'll do the portrait, but it has to be here."

He breathed out a frustrated sigh. He was tired of all the barriers she kept putting up. He'd tried being congenial and generous, but his patience was now razor-thin. They made a verbal agreement, now he expected her to hold up her end of it.

Maybe it was time he be frank with her. Nothing else seemed to be working. "I don't know what is going on with you, but we have an agreement. I expect you to fulfill it. Be ready to go Monday at 6:00 a.m." When she opened her mouth to argue, he said, "I have witnesses to our verbal contract." He gestured to his security team. "Don't push me on this."

Her eyes narrowed. "Now your true colors come out."

He wasn't sure what that meant, but he was beyond caring at this point. He handed over her groceries, plus his own. "Here you go. I will see you tomorrow."

She glanced down at the bags. "But these are your groceries."

"I've lost my appetite. Good evening."

Then he turned to find his car waiting for him. He climbed inside and closed the door. All the while he asked himself why he bothered. If she was that opposed to working for him, why push the subject? Was it his ego? Or was it something more?

In that moment, he didn't want to dissect his emotions. It was enough that she seemed to have finally resigned herself to the fact that they were leaving on Monday. He had a feeling sitting for this portrait wasn't going to be boring. Far from it.

Had that really happened?

She'd agreed to work for the prince?

Indigo replayed the events in her mind as she let herself into the apartment. As she passed the living room, she found her mother had dozed off with her reading glasses on and an open book now resting on her chest.

The money the prince was willing to pay her for the portrait would be enough to get her mother moved into the assisted living center that her mother had chosen. It would make a world of difference to both of them. Her mother would no longer feel like such a burden to her, which wasn't the truth as far as Indigo was concerned. But it was what her mother thought and felt that was important.

With her mother having round-the-clock help, it would give Indigo the freedom to do what she needed to do to expand her career. Her first step in that direction was the gallery showing coming up in two weeks.

That meant she had two weeks to do the preliminary work for the portrait of the prince. It should be enough time. She just hoped he knew that an oil painting would take much longer. It was necessary to allow the paint to dry between layers. It could take her four to six weeks to complete the project. And that would be pushing it, because she had other obligations.

Indigo put away the groceries, including those the prince had given her. Though she opposed handouts, in this case she didn't believe in things going to waste. Then she prepared a selection of vegetables in a light marinara and served it over pasta.

She shared dinner with her mother, who regaled her with what she'd read in her book. Her mother loved books more than anything, but she wasn't opposed to bingeing on a good television series. It was whatever struck her mother at the moment.

"Mama, I need to talk you." She hoped what she had to say wouldn't upset her.

Her mother leaned back in her chair, having finished her meal. Her oxygen cannula helped her breathe. These days it was her constant companion. "You look so serious."

"It's nothing for you to worry about," Indigo said. "It's just that I had this amazing opportunity come up, and I was hoping to take advantage of it."

"It sounds exciting. I'm assuming this has something to do with your gallery show."

She shrugged. "I don't know. We'll see."

Suddenly her mother gave her an idea or two. She could make this trip work for her in more than one way. Though it was too late to put together any more pieces for the showing, it wasn't too late to start on new pieces for the next show. And from what she'd heard from her father and now the prince, Rydiania was one of the most beautiful countries in all of Europe. She might be able to get some photos and sketches that she could work from later. She tucked the thought away for future use.

"What is the opportunity?"

There was no way she was telling her mother the truth. She didn't want to upset her. "I'm going to be traveling around a bit—doing some research for some future paintings."

"When are you leaving?"

"I need to leave Monday. Will that be a problem?"

Her mother frowned. "Sweetie, I don't want to hold you back. That's why I would like to live on my own again."

"And I have good news there. I think we'll be able to get you moved into assisted living when I get back."

Her mother's eyes filled with hope. "What? But how?"

"I've been working with the finances, and between what you have and what I have or will have very soon, we can afford to get you into the place you chose."

Instead of the excitement she expected to see on her mother's face, she frowned. "This isn't what I wanted."

"You don't want to move?" For months, it was all her mother had been talking about.

Her mother shook her head. "It's not that. I just hate having to rely on you. I hate that you have to pay for me to move. It's just not right."

Indigo got to her feet and moved to her mother's side. She knelt down next to her. "You aren't asking me to do this. I'm doing this because I want you to be happy. And I know living here isn't the same as you having your own place. I love you, Mama. Please let me help you with this."

Tears shimmered in her mother's eyes. "How did I get so lucky to have a daughter like you?"

"I'm the one who is lucky to have you." She gave her mother a hug.

When Indigo pulled back, her mother asked. "How long will you be gone?"

"No longer than two weeks, because I have the gallery showing."

Her mother nodded and smiled. "I can't wait to go. I'm so proud of you."

"Thanks, Mama."

It never ever got old hearing that her mother was proud of her—though there were times when Indigo didn't think there was much for her mother to feel proud about. If her mother knew what Indigo was about to do in order to come up with the money for her mother's new living arrangements, she was quite certain her mother would be disappointed in her.

"Did you speak to your aunt yet about stopping by while you're gone?" her mama asked.

"I wanted to speak to you first." And then she remembered all the food in the fridge. "I already stocked the kitchen. It should keep you for a little while. And there are leftovers from tonight."

"I'm not an invalid," her mother insisted.

Her mother was right, but Indigo also knew it didn't take a lot to tire her mother. "I just don't want you overdoing things, is all."

"I won't."

"Famous last words." Indigo sent her mother a smile. "Now what can I do for you before I go?"

"Well, you took care of the shopping, and I just got a new shipment of books and I'll take care of calling your aunt. It'll give her a chance to tell me what's been going on in her life. I think she might be dating someone, but she hasn't told me his name."

"Maybe she's not ready to talk about him yet."

"But she's my sister. She's supposed to tell me everything. I live vicariously through her."

Indigo had known for a long time that her mother had no intentions of finding love again. Even if she wasn't dealing with heart issues, she said that she'd had her one great love and that was enough for her. Indigo wondered what it would be like to have a love like her parents had shared.

Indigo was beginning to wonder if there was a love out there for her. Not that she was looking, because right now she didn't have time for romance. She had too many other responsibilities.

Her mother carried her dishes to the kitchen. Her steps were slow and small, but she didn't let that stop her.

Indigo hated seeing her mother being just a shadow of the strong woman who had buried her husband and raised her teenage daughter alone while working as a reporter. Her mother had been such an amazing role model until her health made her slow down.

And now it was Indigo's turn to do everything she could to make her mother's life as comfortable as possible. Part of that included giving her mother back a semblance of independence—even if it meant going back on a promise to her father to never step foot in Rydiania.

CHAPTER EIGHT

SHE COULDN'T BELIEVE she'd agreed to this.

At exactly six o'clock that morning, a black sedan had pulled up in front of her apartment building. There were no flags to reveal that its passenger was a foreign dignitary. And the windows were tinted, hiding the occupants from her aunt's curious view as she'd passed by on her way into the apartment.

Aunt Aggie paused on the doorstep next to Indigo. "Is the fancy car waiting for you?"

Indigo attempted to act casual. "Yes. I'm off to the airport." Her fingers tightened on the handle of her suitcase. "Thanks for helping out Mama."

"You don't have to thank me. I'm more than happy to help out. Good luck with your project." Aunt Aggie sent her a bright smile, as though she knew what Indigo was up to.

But that wasn't possible. Her gaze moved to the dark sedan to make sure Prince Istvan was still inside. She breathed easier knowing he was hidden from sight behind those dark tinted windows.

"Thank you. I should be going." After a quick hug, Indigo made her way to the waiting car.

The driver got out and opened the door for her as well as took her luggage to stow in the rear. To Indigo's surprise, Istvan wasn't waiting for her inside the sedan. According to his driver, the prince had other matters to attend to and would meet them at the private airport.

Istvan was indeed waiting for her outside the hangar. The crew was ready to go and in no time, they were in the air.

A few hours later, Indigo lounged in a leather seat of the private royal jet, where she'd been staring out at the blue sky. In the rear, the prince's security detail was seated. They were so quiet it was easy to forget they were there.

She glanced over to the side to find Istvan sitting across the aisle with his laptop resting on a table in front of him. He had an earpiece, and he talked in a fast, low voice. His fingers moved rapidly over the keyboard. She couldn't help but wonder what had him so preoccupied. Was it royal business? Or something else?

Whatever kept him so busy had given her time to come to grips with the reality of the situation. She stared out the window at the blue sky dotted with a few puffy white clouds. The earth looked so far away as they grew nearer to her birthplace.

Her palms grew damp as she envisioned coming face-to-face with the king and queen. The idea didn't appeal to her. Not at all. There had to be a way to avoid them. She just needed to give it some more thought.

Ding.

Indigo glanced toward the front of the cabin. She noticed a small seat-belt sign was lit up. This must mean they'd already arrived in Rydiania. She glanced over at Istvan to see if he'd noticed the alert.

"I don't care. I've got other obligations. We'll discuss this later." He withdrew the earpiece and placed it in his pocket. Then he glanced in her direction. "I'm sorry about that."

"No problem." And she meant that sincerely. She wasn't sure what they would have discussed during the four-plus hours they'd been in the air.

"The palace isn't happy that I was away. There's a lot to catch up on."

"I can't even imagine." Which was quite true. When she was a young child, back before her father had been exiled, he had come home late at night after she'd gone to sleep. On the rare times he was home early, he'd tell her tales of the royals. She'd been so young at the time that she'd thought they were fairy tales, but as she grew older, she realized many of the bedtime stories her father had told her had been grounded in reality.

"I take it this is your first visit to Rydiania." His voice interrupted her trip into the past. "I'll see that you have a tour. After all, we can't have you locked away painting the whole time you're here."

"I don't mind working the whole time." The faster she finished her preliminary work, the sooner she'd get back to Greece. And even though her aunt was keeping a close eye on her mother, Indigo didn't want to be gone too long. Since the death of her father, she and her mother had grown even closer than before.

"I insist," Istvan said in a firm tone. "All work and no play, makes Indigo a dull girl."

The fact he knew that saying totally caught her off guard. It sure didn't seem like something a royal would know. It seemed... Well, it seemed so normal. Kind of the way it'd felt when they'd visited the market together.

But Istvan wasn't normal. He was a royal. And not just any royal—a Rydiania prince. And no matter how handsome he was or how kind he could be, she couldn't forget that he was one of them. Only she wasn't like her father—she wasn't going into this blind. She knew how cutthroat the royals could be. And armed with this knowledge, she was protected from being hurt by them.

"Buckle up." His voice drew her from her thoughts.

"Um...what did you say?"

"We're about to land. You'll need to fasten your seat belt."

"Oh. Right." Heat rushed to her cheeks, as he'd

once more distracted her. She couldn't let that happen again. She had to stay focused.

After fastening her seat belt, she turned her head to the lush landscape. The green was periodically dotted with towns. She really wouldn't mind exploring the area. The last time she'd been outside Greece had been to paint in Italy. Her portfolio had needed some diversity, and the trip to Venice had been quite successful.

A smile tugged at her lips. For so long, she'd struggled to get her art career off the ground. Her father had told her to be more practical. Her aunt had tried to hire her at her hair salon. The only one who had believed in her becoming a success had been her mother. She had told Indigo numerous times that she could become anything she set her mind on.

And now, after this assignment, she'd be able to request high fees for her portraits. And her art would go for large enough figures that she'd be able to maintain her mother's care indefinitely. The thought reaffirmed her determination to make the most of this trip.

As the plane began its descent, Indigo gripped the arms of her seat. The plane shook as it hit turbulence. Her body tensed as her fingers dug into the armrests. *We'll be fine. We'll be fine.*

All of the sudden, a warm hand covered hers. She glanced over to find Istvan gazing at her.

He sent her a reassuring smile. "We're almost on the ground."

She nodded, not trusting her voice. And then her gaze darted back toward the window. The fact she'd flown at all was a bit of a miracle. But she'd learned from her father, who had let the world get the best of him, that she couldn't follow his lead. She had to be strong and face life's challenges if she wanted to make it in this world.

"Are you okay?" he asked.

She nodded.

"Was it bad?"

Her gaze swung back around to him. "What?"

"The plane incident—was it bad?"

How did he know? It wasn't like she ever talked about it. In fact, she didn't really want to get into it. But part of overcoming her fear was talking about it.

"It could have been worse." It never escaped her that her life had been spared that day. "I... I was in a near crash a few years back."

He gave her hand a reassuring squeeze. "That would unnerve anyone."

"At first I didn't want to fly ever again, but I realized if I wanted to follow my dreams, flying would be a part of it."

"That was very brave of you."

She shrugged. She didn't feel brave. She felt silly for being afraid to fly, even if she overcame the fear little by little each time she stepped onto a plane.

"I was on a flight home from London." In her mind's eye she was back on that plane. "It had been the usual flight, with the inevitable delay taking off, but then everything settled down. The plane wasn't full, so I had no one beside me and I could relax. I was so anxious to get home. I wanted to tell my mother all about my art classes." It was right when her art career had started to take off.

"That's a long way to go for art lessons." His voice was gentle and not judgmental. It was though he had said enough to prod her to keep telling her story.

"It isn't far to go when you have a rare opportunity to learn from one of the best artists in the world." And then she dropped the name of a well-respected painter and glanced at Istvan to see if he recognized the name.

His eyes widened. "I understand the reason for your trip. Obviously, like me, he saw the true magnificence of your work."

His compliment made her heart beat faster as heat rushed to her cheeks. Was Istvan serious? As she gazed deeply into his blue eyes, she forgot what she'd been thinking. When she realized she'd been staring into his eyes too long, she lowered her gaze. His hand was still covering hers. It made her heart *tap-tap* even faster.

She needed to focus on something besides the prince. She swallowed hard as she prepared to finish her story. "I was gazing out the window, enjoying the sunshine and blue skies. The next thing I knew, there was a strange sound that I later learned was a bird strike, and the engine went out."

The memory of the fire and smoke was so vivid in her mind—just as it had been in her nightmares for a long time after the event. Maybe other people wouldn't have been affected by the event, but she'd felt like she'd been given another chance at life, and she'd promised herself she wouldn't squander it.

She could feel his gaze upon her. "I… I didn't think we were going to make it out alive. Suddenly the plane started to descend quickly. Too quickly."

"No wonder you aren't comfortable on a plane."

"In the end, our amazing pilot made an emergency landing. It was a rough landing, but I was never so happy to step on solid ground in my life."

"And yet you didn't let it stop you."

"I know what happens when you let setbacks and events stop you from living your life." Now why had she gone and said that? She wasn't going to share the tragedy that had befallen her father.

Just then the plane shuddered once more. She turned her head to the window and found they were on the ground. She could at last breathe a bit easier.

The prince withdrew his hand from hers, leaving a noticeably cool spot. "We have arrived."

While the plane taxied to a private hangar, Istvan gathered his things and placed them in his attaché. All Indigo had to grab was her sketch pad that still held nothing but blank pages. Usually she spent her downtime sketching ideas for a new painting, but she'd been utterly distracted on the flight. She told herself it was the flying and not her company that had her distracted.

As the plane rolled to a stop, she glanced out the window to find a dark sedan waiting for them. This time the sedan was larger, and the country's flags adorned the front of the vehicle. A gold crest of the royal family was emblazed on the door. This vehicle was here to whisk them off to the palace.

Her stomach sank down to her heels. "I don't have to stay at the palace," Indigo said. "I'd be fine staying in the village."

Istvan arched a brow. "You are refusing to stay at the palace?"

"I'm just saying that I would be more comfortable staying in the village. I… I'd get a chance to take in the community and the sights."

He studied her for a moment. "If I didn't know better, I'd think you were trying to get away from me."

She was busted. "If that's not acceptable, just say so."

He shrugged. "I'm not going to make you stay at the palace. You just need to be available to work on the portrait starting tomorrow."

"I will."

They moved to the now-open doorway. A man wearing a dark suit and a serious expression stood at the bottom of the steps, waiting to greet the prince. "Your Highness, did you have a good trip?"

"Yes, I did." Istvan glanced over at Indigo as she joined them. "Jozsef, this is Indigo. She's going to be painting my portrait. Indigo, this is Jozsef, my private secretary, who keeps my calendar manageable."

Jozsef's brows ever so briefly lifted before he resumed his neutral expression. "Your Highness, you should know the queen has hired her own artist."

"I'll deal with the queen later. Right now, Ms. Castellanos would like to have accommodations in the village. Could you find her something appropriate?"

"Yes, sir." Jozsef stepped away and made a phone call.

"You didn't have to make him do that." Indigo didn't want to be an imposition. In fact, she was hoping to make her presence less known by staying the village.

"It's no problem. It's Jozsef's job to handle these matters." When they approached the car, the driver opened the door for him. The prince stood back and gestured for her to get in first.

She did as he requested. The interior of the sedan was done up in black, just like the outside of the car. But on the seat in gold thread was the royal family's crest. And the leg space was more generous than in a normal car. There was even a small bar in the back of the front seats and a dividing window to give them some privacy.

When the prince climbed in the back seat and settled next to her, the space seemed to shrink considerably. His arm brushed hers and sent a cascade of goose bumps racing down her arm.

She moved over. The door armrest dug into her side. When she glanced over at Istvan, she found amusement dancing in his eyes.

"You don't have to press yourself against the door." He closed his door. "There's plenty of room for both of us."

The problem was that sitting back here with him was cozy. Too cozy. And she was increasingly aware of how attractive he was, with his broad shoulders, muscular chest and long legs. Her heart pitter-pattered. She swallowed hard.

She needed to remain professional. She laced her fingers together in her lap. "You do understand that I can't complete the painting in the two weeks I'll be here."

He nodded. "I understand. Do you want me to

sit for you tomorrow and you can sketch me or something?"

She shook her head. "I'd like to observe you going about your normal day, if that would be possible."

His brows rose high on his forehead. "You want to watch me work?"

She nodded. "If possible."

"It's certainly possible, but it sounds boring." He sent her a smile.

She noticed the way his lips parted, revealing his straight white teeth. There was a dimple in his cheek that made him even cuter. And when the smile reached his blue eyes, they twinkled.

She subdued a sigh. No one had a right to be that handsome. And try as she might not to like him, she was failing miserably. She'd found absolutely nothing to dislike about him. Was it possible he was nothing at all like his parents? Hope swelled in her chest.

"So why did you hire me if the queen already has someone to do your portrait?"

"Because it's my portrait, and I want to pick who paints it. My country needs a fresh approach. I'm hoping with your help they will see me in a new light and not part of the same old regime that has been running the country in the exact same manner for much too long."

Wow! She really had misjudged him, hadn't she? Her hope was so great that it surprised her.

It wasn't like she was going to let herself fall for him. Not a chance. But she hoped he was different for, um, his country. Yes, that was it. His country could use new leadership. Because it didn't really matter to her personally if he was the same or different. Not at all.

CHAPTER NINE

PERHAPS THIS HAD been a miscalculation.

Istvan had noticed how Indigo made sure to leave a lot of space between them, whether it was on the jet or now in the back seat of the car. What had made her so jumpy around him?

He wanted to ask her, but he didn't dare. As it was, their conversation was finally getting her to relax a bit. And he didn't want to stop talking because the more she relaxed, the more he saw the part of her that had first attracted him to her. Not that he was expecting or even wanting anything to come of this arrangement—other than an impressive portrait that would put his unique stamp on his upcoming reign.

"You just need to tell me what you'll need while you're here," he said.

"Need?"

"Yes. What art supplies will you need?"

"Oh. Okay." She reached in her purse and pulled out a slip of paper. She held it out to him. "Here you go."

He was duly impressed that she was this organized. He glanced down at the list. "I'll see that these items are brought to you."

"Thank you."

Tap-tap.

Istvan opened the window. Jozsef stood there. He leaned down and spoke softly into Istvan's ear. There was no room available in the village. It would seem Indigo would be staying at the palace after all.

He put up the window and turned to Indigo. "It would appear there's a wedding celebration in the village and all the rooms are taken."

"Oh." Disappointment showed in her eyes.

Just then the car engine started, and they began to move. Istvan leaned back in his seat. "Don't worry. You'll like the palace. It's a cross between a home and a museum."

She smiled at him.

"What did I say that was so amusing?"

"I've just never heard anyone describe their home as a museum."

He shrugged. "It has a collection of art from the past and some from the present. Every time a foreign dignitary visits the palace, they feel obligated to bring a gift. So there's quite a collection. Except in my wing."

"You have your own wing of the palace?"

He nodded. "It's one of the benefits of being the crown prince. My siblings all share a wing.

And then my parents have their own wing. And that leaves one wing for visiting guests."

"And here all I have is a two-bedroom apartment. It could probably fit in just one room in the palace."

When she sent him a playful smile, he let out a laugh. The more she relaxed, the more he liked her. She reminded him of his younger sister Cecilia. They were both free spirits and full of energy. He had a feeling if they had a chance, they would be fast friends. And then maybe he'd have an excuse to see Indigo again.

She wanted to hate Rydiania.

She wanted it to be the ugliest place on the earth. But instead, she found it to be one of the most beautiful places she'd ever been.

Indigo stared out the window at the tall green trees lining each side of the smooth roadway. When the trees parted, there was a lush meadow with a large pond. Upon the placid water were ducks—a mama and seven ducklings. Inwardly she sighed. If she didn't know better, she'd swear Istvan had created this scene to impress her—not that he had any reason to want to do such a thing.

And yet Indigo felt as though they were driving through a watercolor painting. This wasn't fair. There had to be something about this place that she hated.

Her gaze hungrily took it all in. The roadway

wove through the country, and for a moment she felt like she was on holiday and had just landed in paradise. Then she decided that the problem with this place was that it was too rural, with its endless green grass, its abundance of wildlife and array of wildflowers. After all, that stuff was nice if you were an outdoorsy person, but she preferred the hubbub of neighborhoods and shops.

And still she kept her face turned toward the window, memorizing all she saw. She told herself that she kept staring because the alternative would be facing Istvan. She wasn't ready for that. Sketching his striking image with his kissable mouth was one thing, but dealing with him on a personal level was quite another.

"What do you think?" he asked.

Did he know her thoughts had drifted back to him? Totally impossible. She just had to keep her wits about her. She couldn't let him know how easily he distracted her.

She gave a small, nonchalant shrug. "It's great if you're a nature fanatic."

He let out a laugh. "I take it you're not into nature."

Why did he insist on making conversation? It wasn't like they were going to become friends. This was a business arrangement. Period. At the end of these two weeks, they'd never see each other again. She'd return to Greece to complete the portrait and then ship it to him. And yet she found herself wanting to talk to him, because he made it so easy to carry on a conversation.

She shrugged. "Honestly, it's beautiful. I'm just used to spending time in a more urban setting."

He nodded. "I understand."

She felt as though she'd said something wrong. She hadn't meant to. "But if I loved a more rustic life, this would definitely be a lovely place to live."

"Have you always lived in Athens?"

She turned her head toward him. "You don't know? I mean, I figured you ran a background check before hiring me."

"Of course. It's a matter of practice for all hires, but that doesn't mean I actually reviewed the entire report. I just made sure you weren't a criminal. And my private secretary rang your employer. Was there something you were expecting me to see?"

She shook her head. She wasn't ready to dredge up the past. "As far back as I can remember, I've lived in Athens."

"That's a long time."

"Hey, did you just call me old?"

His brows rose. "What?" Worry reflected in his eyes. "No. Of course not."

She sent him a playful smile. Who knew it was so easy to undo the prince's calm, cool exterior? "Uh-huh."

"Do you have a lot of family?"

"I have my mother. My father, well, he died when I was a teenager." Why had she gone and brought up her father? She never discussed him with anyone but her mother. And even then it was about his life, never his death.

"I'm so sorry."

She shrugged off his sympathy, refusing to acknowledge the pain she felt when she thought of the life that had been cut much too short. "It was a long time ago."

"Do you have any siblings?"

She shook her head. Tired of talking about herself, she decided to turn the tables. "And how about you? Any siblings?"

"I have three sisters."

She tried to imagine him as a child with three younger sisters chasing after him. "Your childhood must have been interesting."

He sighed. "You have no idea. My sisters can be a handful. You'll get to meet them while you're here."

"I look forward to it." Did she? Or had she just uttered those words out of habit? She wasn't sure—she wasn't sure about a lot of things lately.

She turned back toward the window. The car wound through the lush valley. Indigo found herself captivated by the majestic scenery. Her fingers twitched with the need to reach for her pencils and sketch pad. But there wasn't time. All of nature's beauty passed by the window far too quickly. Instead she reached for her phone to snap some photos.

Istvan cleared his throat. "I like to think that Rydiania is one of the most beautiful places on the planet. I hope you'll get a chance to do some exploring while you're here."

The idea appealed to her, but she needed to remain focused on her work. "We don't have much time together. I really need to do the groundwork for your portrait."

He nodded. "I understand."

The car slowed as it approached a more urban area. She gazed forward, finding high-rises and a sea of concrete buildings. *A city? Here? Really?*

But then the car turned to the left and completely diverted around the city. "We're not going to visit the city?"

"You sound disappointed."

She shrugged. "I'm just curious to see what a city in Rydiania looks like, especially one that is surrounded by a forest."

"I'll make sure we plan an excursion so you can explore. There's an arts section to the city that I'm sure you'll be interested in. But right now, I'm expected at a meeting at the palace."

"Of course." It was far too easy to forget that he was a prince and not just a commoner, like herself. She would have to be more careful going forward.

A peaceful silence settled over the car as it carried them closer to the palace. She had to admit that she was curious to see it in person. The pictures she'd seen online were striking. She wondered if it was really that impressive or if the pictures had received some touch-ups.

More houses came into view. They were separated by expansive property. Most yards were meticulously cared for with short grass, trimmed bushes and brightly colored flowers from yellow to pinks and reds.

They slowed to a stop and then merged into a single roadway that wound its way into a small village. It was filled with what she imagined were tourists. Some had brochures in their hands. Others had their phones out and were snapping pictures of the rustic storefronts.

This place, with its many unique shops and amazing aromas, from buttery cinnamon to herbs and vegetables, permeated the car. Indigo found herself inhaling deeply. "Something sure smells good."

Istvan smiled. "Oh, yes, there are many wonderful places to eat in the village."

Her stomach rumbled in agreement. "I'll definitely keep that in mind. Is the palace far from here?"

"Not at all. In fact it's just on the other side of the village."

Her stomach knotted. Even though she had agreed to come here to help her mother, she felt as though she were betraying her father. Would he understand her decision? She hoped so.

The car slowed, drawing Indigo's attention. She focused on the very tall wrought iron gate in front of the car. Guards in deep purple uniforms with black hats stood in front of the gate. To either side of the gate were black guard shacks that were much more than shacks, because no shack looked that nice.

With precise movements that must have been practiced for many, many hours, they moved in unison and swung the giant gates open. As the car proceeded along the smoothly paved roadway, Indigo's heart raced and she clutched her hands together.

And there before them stood a gigantic palace. It was built out of a light gray stone. Impressive turrets stood at the corners. Atop the palace fluttered a purple-and-white flag. The car swung around and pulled to a stop beneath a portico. The doors were swung open by gentlemen dressed formally in black-and-white suits.

"Welcome to my home." Istvan sent her a reassuring smile.

She opened her mouth, but no words would come out. What was she supposed to say? *It's beautiful?* Because, well, it was the most magnificent *home* she'd ever seen. Or was she supposed to be unimpressed, as this was the home of the people who had hurt her father so deeply?

She pressed her lips back together. Nothing felt quite right.

And so she was quietly led up the few steps to the red runner that led them inside the palace. No matter how much she wanted to hate this place, she couldn't deny the flutter in her chest as she took in its magnificence. *Just... Wow!*

If she hadn't seen all this for herself, she never would have believed it. Because the pictures online didn't come close to doing the palace justice—not one little bit.

It was like stepping into the pages of a storybook—the kind her mother read to her when she was a child. Sunlight streamed into the round foyer through a giant glass dome three stories up from where they stood. The sun's rays lit up the room and gave it a glow. It was though she were standing in a very special place.

"Indi, are you coming?" Istvan called from where he stood on the grand steps that were lined with a deep purple carpet that led to the second floor.

"Indi?" It was the first time he'd called her that, and she wasn't sure how she felt about him using the nickname.

He smiled. "Has no one ever called you that?"

"Um…yes. My friends do."

"Good. It suits you. I'll show you to your room."

As she made her way up the steps, she couldn't

help but wonder what had just happened. Was the prince saying he wanted to be friends with her? If so, how did she feel about him taking such liberties? But was it worth her getting worked up over a nickname? Probably not.

Istvan didn't have airs about him like she'd imagined a member of a royal family having. He was down-to-earth. And dare she admit it…if he were anyone else, she would be totally into him.

Still, he was the crown prince of the country that had played a role in the loss of her father. She couldn't ever let herself forget that, no matter how sexy she found his smile or how she could let herself get lost in his dreamy eyes.

When she smiled, she stole the breath from his lungs.

He hadn't felt this alive and invigorated in a long time.

Istvan was certain he'd made the right decision to bring Indi here. She was like a breath of fresh air in this stodgy old palace. He needed someone like her around to remind him of how things could be in the kingdom if the harsh traditions that had been carried on generation after generation were to be replaced with a gentler and more modern way of doing things.

He was going to be the change for his family. He knew his radical ideas would be met with resistance. He just hoped he had the strength to see change brought to this country that was stuck in the ways of the past.

And his first way of showing his country that his reign would be different—that *he* was different—was in his formal portrait. Indi would take his idea of change and make it a visual statement.

They climbed the many steps and paused at the top. He wanted to give Indi a chance to look around and gain her bearings. Not everyone was used to living in a palace. Even though he had grown up within these massive walls, he realized it didn't hold the warmth and coziness that other homes did. He supposed there were trade-offs for everything in life.

His three sisters strode toward them. What were the three of them doing together? On second thought, he didn't want to know. Their eyes lit up when they noticed Indi at his side. In fact, they hardly paid him any attention. He groaned inwardly. His sisters could be quite overbearing when they thought he was interested in someone. Not that he was interested in Indi in a romantic way. At this point in his life, he didn't have time for a relationship.

The three princesses came to a stop in front of him. Gisella and Beatrix were dressed in blouses, pants and heels, while his youngest sister, Cecilia, wore a light blue skirt that barely made it to her midthigh and a pale-yellow halter top.

"Who's your friend?" his eldest sister, Princess Gisella, asked.

He glanced at Indi, who looked curious to meet the princesses. "Indigo, these are my sisters." He gestured to the left. "This is Princess Gisella. She is the oldest. Next to her is my youngest sister, Princess Cecilia. And next to her is Princess Beatrix."

"It's nice to meet you all," Indigo said.

His sisters all wore their well-practiced smiles. They could be so friendly and welcoming when they wanted to be, but they could also become defensive and freeze out people. He had absolutely no idea how they were going to react to Indi. He hoped they would give her a chance.

And then his sisters all spoke at once. Each fired off questions at Indigo, who looked surprised and overwhelmed. His sisters could be like a force of nature when you had to deal with all of them at once—at least that's what his father often said. And Istvan had to agree with him.

"Stop!" His firm tone drew his sisters' attention. "Let Indigo get situated before you bombard her with questions."

Gisella narrowed her gaze on him. "Does Mother know about this?"

"No." He chose not to add any further explanation.

Gisella crossed her arms and frowned at him.

"She's not going to like you bringing home an unexpected guest."

His other sisters nodded in agreement.

"She's not a guest. Not like you're thinking. Indigo is an artist. She's here to paint my portrait."

Surprised looks filtered across all the princesses' faces. So they really thought he was bringing home a girlfriend for his family to meet? That would be the last thing he would do with someone he was romantically interested in. His family could be intimidating on a good day, and on a bad day, well… He didn't want to think about it.

"Is that true about you being an artist?" Cecilia asked.

Indigo nodded. "It is. We met when I did a sketch of your brother."

"That sounds interesting," Beatrix said. "Where was this?"

"Stop," Istvan said. "Indigo is tired from traveling."

"Istvan, is that you?" the queen's voice trailed up the staircase.

He turned to the stairs, expecting to see his mother, but she was still downstairs. "Yes. I'm home."

The click of heels on the foyer's marble floor could be heard approaching the stairs. He turned back to his sisters. All he saw was their backs as they all headed in different directions. So much for them helping him manage his mother so she didn't frighten Indigo away.

He leaned over to Indigo and said softly, "Don't worry."

"I'm not." Her tone was firm as she straightened her shoulders.

Most people were intimidated when they first met the king or queen. That didn't appear to be the case with Indigo. Interesting.

"Istvan, there you are." The queen stepped onto the landing.

He turned his attention to his mother as she headed toward them. She wore a conservative navy dress with white trim, and near the neckline was her diamond-and-amethyst royal brooch in the shape of a crown. Both of his parents wore their pins daily. He was supposed to wear a similar one since he was heir to the throne, but he found it pretentious. He picked and chose the days he wore his royal pin.

"Hello, Mother." He stepped forward and gave her a feathery kiss upon the cheek.

"It's about time you returned."

He noticed how her gaze moved to Indi, and instead of a surprised look, she assumed her well-rehearsed smile. He knew that smile. It was one of duty that never reached his mother's eyes. She used it as a shield to hide what she was really feeling.

And since he had not advised his mother that

he would be bringing home a visitor, he was certain she had been caught off guard—something she hated. His mother liked to know about everything before it happened.

"Mother, I'd like to introduce you to Indigo Castellanos of Athens, Greece. Indigo, I'd like to introduce you to Queen Della."

He noticed how Indi froze. She didn't smile. She didn't do the customary curtsy to the queen. She didn't move. It reminded him of their first meeting. Maybe he should have given her a heads-up on what was expected when first meeting the king or queen. But he'd been distracted by Indi's presence and his excitement to spend the next couple of weeks with her.

An awkward moment passed before the queen said, "Welcome."

He noticed the muscles of Indi's throat work. "Thank you for having me in your...home."

The queen continued to study Indi.

"Mother, I've hired Indi...um, Indigo to paint my formal portrait."

This time his mother couldn't hide her surprise. Her penciled brows rose. "We already have an artist. He's done other royal paintings."

"Not this one." His voice held a firmness. He wasn't going to change his plans. If he backed down now, his mother would always walk over him and his plans. He couldn't be an effective ruler that way.

The queen's eyes grew dark, but when she spoke, her agitation was veiled. "The king is looking for you."

"Is he in the blue room?" It was his father's favorite room in the palace. Though it wasn't the king's formal office, it was the room he used most to conduct his business.

"Yes. He's expecting you to meet with him immediately."

He was not going to abandon Indigo, whose face had gone distinctly pale. "I will see Father shortly." And with that he turned to Indigo. "Shall we?"

Indigo continued to stare at the queen, but he wasn't able to read her thoughts. To say their first meeting hadn't gone well would be a total understatement. The queen turned and made her way down the steps. Indigo watched until she was out of sight.

He gently took ahold of her arm. "Shall we?"

She blinked and looked at him. "What?"

He grew concerned about her. "Are you all right?"

She nodded. "I'm sorry. I...uh, was lost in thought for a moment."

He wasn't sure he believed her. By her pale complexion and the gaze of her eyes, it was almost as though she'd seen a ghost.

Indie walked beside him. Maybe he was just overthinking things. After all, they'd had a busy day of travel, and then meeting the queen without any forewarning or guidance on their customs must have caught her a little off guard. He would have to do better in the future.

CHAPTER TEN

THAT HADN'T GONE quite as she'd thought.

Many times over the years, Indigo had imagined one day facing the king and queen of Rydiania. In none of her fantasies had she stood there silently. That was the second time she'd been rendered silent upon meeting a member of the royal family. What was wrong with her?

She wasn't one to keep quiet when something bothered her. So then why had she been so quiet upon meeting the queen?

Maybe it was the fact that she had hoped the queen would recognize her—that she'd apologize for banishing her father, for ruining his life. Not that Indigo ever really thought any of that would happen.

There was a bit of satisfaction in the fact that the daughter of the man who'd been banished from the kingdom was now an invited guest of the palace. Yes, indeed, it felt good. Although it didn't come close to offsetting the pain and destruction that the royal family had caused hers. And for what? So they could eliminate any threat to them claiming the throne for themselves?

She'd felt a rush of so many emotions on her first night in the palace that she'd begged off on joining the royal family for dinner. She pleaded a headache, which wasn't far from the truth. A tray of food had been sent to her room.

The following morning, Istvan had given her the grand tour of the palace. Her favorite rooms had been the library, with its many bookcases and comfy couches, and the conservatory, with its walls of windows and dozens of plants.

Others would probably have been awed by the throne room or the flag room, but they did nothing for her. She was actually curious about the kitchen, but the tour didn't include that room. She wondered, if a royal got hungry in the middle of the night, did they slip down to the kitchen to get a snack? Or did they have someone to do it for them? She decided it was probably the latter.

As evening settled on her second day in the palace, she was alone in her room. She turned around, taking in the spacious room that could easily fit her apartment. Right now, her home seemed a million miles away. She'd just spoken to her mother, who was enjoying Aunt Aggie's company. Indigo missed them both.

It was time to dress for dinner. She decided

to shower. It had been a long day, and a shower would make her feel refreshed. Istvan had said he would be by to pick her up at seven.

She wasn't exactly sure how to dress. Obviously jeans and a T-shirt were out. And so she picked a peach-pink maxi dress. She blew her long hair dry and then pulled it up into a ponytail, pulling loose curls to soften her face.

As for makeup, she didn't usually wear much, which was probably odd considering she was an artist. But she very rarely wore heavy eye makeup or bold lipsticks. Tonight she would do what she normally did. The more she stuck with her usual routine, the more relaxed she'd be.

She applied foundation, followed by powder. She indulged in some glittery sand-tone eyeshadow and mascara. And on her lips, she applied a frosted beige gloss. Okay, so maybe it was more than her normal, but it wasn't too much. She wondered what Istvan would think.

As soon as she realized that she cared at all what he thought of her, she banished the thought. She was here for work, nothing more.

Knock-knock.

Her heart started to race. She sensed Istvan standing on the other side of the door. And suddenly this evening was feeling much more like a date than a business dinner. Perhaps she should have opted for the jeans, but even she knew that would be utterly unacceptable for dinner with the royal family.

"Coming." She glanced in the mirror one last time.

Considering she was having dinner in the palace, she realized her outfit was a bit on the casual side. Perhaps she should have brought something more formal, but then again, she didn't really own anything fit for palace living.

She moved to the door and opened it. Standing on the other side of the door was Prince Istvan. She could tell he had recently showered, as his dark hair was still a bit damp.

Wow! She swallowed hard. His collared shirt had the first few buttons undone, giving the slightest glimpse of his tanned, muscular chest. Her gaze skimmed down to his dark jeans. Jeans? So the royals did wear jeans around the palace, just like normal people. *Interesting.*

"Are you ready to go?" He smiled at her.

So she'd been busted checking him out. Her mouth grew dry, and she struggled to swallow. She had to keep it together. She didn't want him to know how much his presence got to her. That wouldn't be good. Not good at all.

"Yes, I am. I hope I'm dressed all right for dinner." Now, why had she gone and said that? It wasn't like she was looking for approval from anyone.

His smile broadened. "You look beautiful."

His compliment made her heart flutter in her chest. "Thank you."

He presented his arm to her. "Shall we?"

She considered ignoring the gesture, but she didn't want to be rude. So far on this trip Istvan had been nothing but kind and generous. He was making it impossible to dislike him. In fact, she was starting to wonder if she had been wrong about him. The thought startled her.

Instead of guiding her to the front stairs that they'd used when they'd first arrived, he turned and headed in the opposite direction. It must be the back way to the dining room.

Her stomach shivered with nerves. Perhaps she should have pleaded another headache in order to get out of this dinner, too. Yes, that would have been a good idea. Would they believe she had a headache for her entire visit? Probably not.

They descended a more modest set of steps. Her stomach was full of butterflies. There was no way she was going to be able to eat. Not a chance.

When they reached the landing, instead of heading into the center of the palace, Istvan led her to an exterior door, where a guard bid them a good evening.

"I don't understand," she said. "Aren't we having dinner in the palace?"

He pushed the door open to a warm summer evening. He paused to look at her. "Is that what you want?"

"No." The word popped out before she realized it.

He smiled at her. "I didn't think so. I have something else in mind."

She should probably ask about the alternate plan, but she decided it didn't really matter to her. If it meant not having to sit across from the king and queen, she was fine with whatever he planned.

The late-summer sun hung low in the sky, sending splashes of pink and purple through the clear sky. Rydiania certainly had the most beautiful sunsets. Just as she was about to mention it, Istvan came to a stop next to a low-slung cherry-red convertible.

He opened the door for her. "I thought you'd like a ride to dinner rather than trying to walk into the village in those."

She glanced down at her heeled sandals. When she'd chosen them, she'd thought she would be walking down the stairs to the palace's dining room. Her gaze lifted to meet his. "You're right. They aren't good to walk long distances in."

"No problem. I haven't had this car out for a spin in a while. So it'll help us both."

She lowered herself to the buttery-soft leather seat. Istvan closed her door, and then he circled around to the driver's seat. It was then that she noticed just how compact the interior was, because when Istvan settled in his seat, his broad shoulders brushed up against hers. Just the casual touch set her stomach aflutter. She slid closer to the door. It was best to keep her distance—at least whatever distance the car allowed them.

He didn't seem to notice their contact or the fact that she'd moved away from him. If he did notice, he certainly didn't let on. Well, if he wasn't going to be affected by their closeness, neither was she.

She focused her gaze straight ahead as he started the car. The engine purred like a fine-tuned machine. Then the tires rolled silently over the paved drive. There was nothing about the palace that wasn't pure perfection, from the manicured green lawn to the impeccably trimmed bushes to the stunning flower gardens with purple, red and white blooms. Quite honestly, no matter what she thought of the royal family, she couldn't deny that she felt as though she were driving through a painting.

"You seemed really interested in the village when we passed through it," he said. "I thought we would dine there. But if you would rather, we could drive into the city. It isn't that much farther."

She would like to explore the city, but that would mean more time alone with Istvan in this impossibly small car. And if she were to lean her head to the side and inhale deeply—not that she had any intention of doing such a thing—but if she were to do it, she knew she would smell his unique masculine scent mingled with soap. Her pulse started to race. It was quite an intoxicating combination. Again, she wasn't going there. Not at all.

"The village is fine." Did her voice sound funny? A little deep and throaty? She swallowed hard. "It...it's beautiful here."

"I agree but then again, I might be a bit biased."

When she glanced over at him, she noticed the smile that hinted at his perfectly white, straight teeth. It was just one more thing that was perfect about him. Not that she was keeping track.

"I'm surprised you spend so much time away from here." She needed to keep the conversation going in order to keep her thoughts from straying.

She could feel his gaze briefly flick to her. "You've been checking up on me?"

"Uh, no. I mean, I just wanted to know a little more about you before I took the assignment. And the internet showed that you travel quite a bit."

He was quiet for a moment, and she started to wonder if he was going to respond. It was obviously no secret that he traveled all of Europe regularly. The press covered his every move—and every single woman he dined with. She ignored the uneasiness she'd felt at glancing at the picture of him with all those beautiful, glamorous women. It also made her wonder why there wasn't press surrounding the palace or lining the street as they made their way into the village.

"I do like to travel." He didn't expand on his reason for being out of the country so much.

The car slowed as they entered the village. The roads were narrow, with vehicles parked on either side. They stopped numerous times to allow people to cross the road. Indigo couldn't help but wonder if the people recognized the prince's car. After all, there were no royal flags on the hood or gold coat of arms on the doors as there were on other royal vehicles.

If the villagers did recognize the car or him behind the wheel, they didn't let on. Sure some smiled and waved, but it wasn't any different than if an ordinary citizen such as herself had stopped for them. Interesting. Even more interesting was that Istvan didn't expect any royal treatment. He was definitely different than she'd imagined. But how different? That was still to be determined.

A relaxing dinner.

And a chance to spend some one-on-one time with Indigo.

Istvan was quite pleased with himself for coming up with a legitimate excuse to avoid a stuffy, strained meal with his parents and siblings. He was certain to hear more about hiring a "nobody" to do his formal portrait.

He'd already been given disapproving looks,

not only from the queen but also from the king when he'd met with him before picking up Indigo for dinner. His father wasn't happy with him. Not all. And then his sister Gisella had sighed at him and asked the same question she always asked him: *Why can't you just do your part?*

His sister made it sound like he should just go along with whatever his parents expected of him. That was never going to happen. He was not a yes man. Never had been. Never would be.

His intent was to bring about a more modern Rydiania. Though the more he strove to move in that direction, the more resistance he encountered. Was he the only one that realized if they didn't loosen the reins, their position as leaders of the kingdom would be in great jeopardy?

He slowed for a car just pulling out and then proceeded into the now-vacant parking spot. "Anything you are particularly hungry for?"

Indigo shook her head. "I'm curious to try some of the local cuisine."

"Then you've come to the right place. No other place cooks Rydianian cuisine quite the way they do here."

"It sounds like you come here often."

"I do." He noticed how her warm brown eyes briefly widened. "I try to spend as much time in the village as possible."

"Isn't that difficult? You know, with you being

the prince and everything. Don't people constantly want pictures and autographs?"

He shook his head. "It's a small village, and the locals all know me. There's no need for them to treat me different. I don't expect it, and they know it. But when the tourists spot me, it can get a bit lively. Thankfully, the village usually quiets down in the evening, when most tourists return to the city."

"Interesting."

"You sound surprised."

"I am. I just—I don't know—thought you spent all your time in the palace."

"My parents do—for the most part. But I don't see how you can govern a country appropriately when you aren't out among the people finding out what's important to them. Come on." He climbed out of the car.

By the time he rounded the front of the car to open the door for Indi, she already had it open and was standing on the sidewalk. He couldn't help but smile. He loved her independent spirit. She didn't stand on traditions or formalities. He needed someone like her in his life—someone to remind him that he wasn't all that different from the people of Rydiania.

Not that he was planning to keep Indi in his life. He knew her life was back in Greece. And his future was all about the next steps for him to step up as king. Even though he'd been groomed for the position ever since his uncle had abdicated the throne, it was still a daunting challenge.

As they strolled along the sidewalk, villagers smiled and said hello in passing. Most of the people were familiar faces to him.

"They're all so nice," Indi said.

"They definitely are." He felt lucky to be a part of this village. It wasn't the same for him in the big city. He only traveled there with heightened security. Here in the village, his security hung back a bit.

Indi gazed at the quaint shops lining both sides of the street. "This village is so cute. I want to grab my pad and pencil to sketch out the scenes."

Her enjoyment of the village pleased him. He pointed to a shop on the street corner. "See that place? They bake the most amazing cinnamon rolls with a buttery frosting. It practically melts in your mouth." He moved his finger to the left. "And over there is a bookstore with every genre imaginable. There are so many bookshelves that it's like making your way through a maze." He continued to provide details about the many storefronts.

"I'm already falling in love with this place." She glanced around the village with big eyes, like those of a child who was set loose in a great big toy store.

They turned a corner. Right across the street was

something he knew would spark Indi's interest—an art gallery. He waited for her to spot it.

Indi gasped as she came to a stop. "You have an art gallery, too?"

"We do. Would you like to have a look?"

"I definitely would." She hesitated. "But we have plans for dinner."

"Plans are made to be changed." He wasn't in any hurry to see the evening end—even if his father wanted to have a meeting about new responsibilities that were being transferred to him. All that could wait. Right now, he was more interested in getting to know Indi. He wanted to know everything about her.

She turned to him. "You'd really do that?"

"I would. Let's go."

"As tempting as that is, I'm afraid that if I go in there, we'll miss dinner completely."

"No problem. I'll just have them prepare some takeaway meals."

Surprise lit up in her eyes. "Are you always this accommodating to your portrait artists?"

He let out a laugh. "No. Definitely not."

She smiled at him. It was a smile that started on her glossy lips and lifted her cheeks until it reached her eyes and made them sparkle like fine gems. It swept his breath away. And for a moment, his gaze dipped back down to her mouth. He wondered what she would do if he were to lean over and press his lips to hers.

He had gone into this arrangement intent on keeping things businesslike, but now he was wondering if that had been an error on his part. It had been so long since he'd enjoyed someone's company this much. Perhaps they could mix a little business with a whole lot of pleasure. Oh, yes, that sounded perfect.

He started to lean toward her.

"Istvan, look at that!" Her excitement drew him from his thoughts.

He immediately straightened and gave himself a mental shake. What was he doing? Indi didn't strike him as the casual-relationship type. If she were, it would have happened by now. And he didn't want to do anything that would end up hurting Indi. She was too kind, and in her eyes he saw pain. Someone had hurt her in the past, and he didn't want to do anything to add to that.

He looked to the left and spotted what had gotten Indi so excited. Moving slowly up the road was a horse and wagon. It wasn't an uncommon sight.

"Some of the local farmers believe in doing things the old way." Much like his father believed change had no place in Rydiania. "They bring their goods into the village in their wagons."

"I love it." She retrieved her phone and snapped some photos.

While she watched the chestnut mare, Istvan

watched her. He had a feeling his life was going to be a lot emptier when she left next week.

"Istvan?" Indi sent him a puzzled look. "Did you hear me?"

"Sorry. I was just thinking about—" he hastily grabbed the first excuse that came to him "—a meeting I'm supposed to have later this evening."

Her brows drew together. "We don't have to go to dinner if you have someplace else to be."

"Don't you worry. I'm exactly where I want to be." He sent her a reassuring smile. And then he presented his arm to her. "Shall we go have a bite to eat? It's just a little farther."

She hesitated, and then she placed her hand in the crook of his arm. "Let's do it."

"Maybe tomorrow we can come back so you can explore the gallery to your heart's content." And then he recalled that his calendar was busy the rest of the week. "On second thought, we'll have to do it next week. I just recalled that we'll be hosting some important guests the rest of the week."

"Oh. I understand. I could return to Greece if this isn't a good time to work on the portrait?"

"No. Stay. We'll make it work. I just won't be able to make any excursions until after our guests have departed. But then I promise a trip to the gallery."

She turned her head and lifted her chin until their gazes met. "I'd like that."

There was this funny feeling in his chest—something he'd never experienced before. It was a warm sensation that radiated from the center outward. And when she turned away, he wanted to draw her attention back to him. Yet he resisted the urge.

He had to stay focused on the preparation for the transition of power—on establishing his own working relationships with influential business-people in Rydiania. His father's health wasn't the best, and they wanted to transfer power while he was still in physically decent shape. To wait until he was frail would put the kingdom in peril. No one wanted that.

But Istvan wasn't anxious for the transition to happen. He had a lot of mixed feelings about it. First, he hated that his father was ill and had to step down. Second, he wasn't sure how he felt about his parents looking over his shoulder while he was on the throne. He knew they wouldn't approve of the changes he wanted to bring to the kingdom—the changes the kingdom needed to see it through another century and beyond.

He halted his thoughts as the restaurant came into sight. A carved red-and-black sign hung above the door.

"L'Artiste Bistro." Her voice held a note of awe. She turned to him. "What's it like?"

He pulled the door open for her. "See for yourself."

She rushed inside to have a look around. Her eyes lit up as she took in all the art, from the mixed-media wall hangings to the busts on pedestals to the plants that were also works of art.

"This place is like a museum." She continued to glance around.

"I thought you would like it. The owner is the sister of the man who owns the art gallery. They decided to combine their talents, and L'Artiste Bistro was born."

"I love it." She smiled brightly.

At that moment, the maître d' spotted them and rushed over to seat them. Instead of requesting his usual table in the back corner of the restaurant, where he was less likely to be spotted by tourists, Istvan decided to sit in the center of the restaurant, where Indi would have a better view of all the art.

After they were seated, she continued to take in the vast amount of artwork. "I feel like I should get up and tour the restaurant."

"Feel free, to but you might want to order first."

She shook her head. "I don't think so."

"Why not?"

"Because…" She glanced around at the other tables. "I don't want to make a scene."

"It's okay. You won't be the first or last to admire the fine artwork."

"Maybe I will after dinner."

As they were handed menus, he realized he

was no longer hungry—at least not for food. His gaze strayed over the top of the menu to Indi, who was busy reviewing all the wonderful dishes being offered.

The only thing he desired in that moment was to learn more about the intriguing woman sitting across from him. She was like a real-life work of art, from her silky hair that made his fingers tingle to reach out and comb through her loose curls to her delicate face that he longed to caress. And then there were her lips—*oh, that mouth.* It begged to be kissed. And if there wasn't a table sitting between them, he might have done exactly that.

CHAPTER ELEVEN

THE FOOD WAS DIVINE.

The decor was amazing.

But the company was sublime.

Indigo couldn't believe she admitted that about Istvan. He was supposed to be the enemy, but the more time she spent with him, the more she found herself enjoying their time together.

He was fun. He was thoughtful. And he was compassionate.

How was it possible Istvan was part of a family that could so coldly and meanly disown their own family member, as well as the staff? It baffled her. There was a lot more to Istvan than she'd ever imagined possible.

And there was the fact that he'd brought her here to do his portrait. In his world, she was an unknown artist—an untested talent. And yet he was willing to stand up to his parents and insist on using her services over those of an established artist. It was the biggest compliment anyone had ever paid her.

The evening had gone by far too quickly, and now they were driving back to the palace. She glanced over at Istvan. In the glow of the dash lights, she watched as he skillfully worked the manual transmission as though it were an extension of his body. He maneuvered the sports car easily over the winding road. With great effort, she forced her gaze straight ahead. She didn't want to be caught staring at him.

And then they were pulling into the palace drive. She suppressed a sigh that the evening was over. She wanted to hear more about him, about his travels. Throughout dinner she had been busy answering his questions about her career and how she'd ended up at the Ludus Resort.

At first, she'd been hesitant to tell him too much about herself. She'd thought it would make her feel vulnerable. But Istvan was very laid-back, yet appropriately engaging. He didn't make her feel awkward. Talking to him, well, it was like talking to an old friend.

As the car slowed and they moved toward the back of the palace, she chanced another glance at him. He was a complex man. He was more than a prince, a brother, a dutiful son and an heir to a throne. He was caring and funny. He could even make jokes about himself. Somehow she couldn't imagine his mother laughing at herself—not a chance. She wondered if the king was more like Istvan.

The car pulled to a stop beneath a big tree. "And we're home."

She let out a small laugh.

"What's so funny?"

"You describing this grand palace as a home."

He arched a brow. "Is it not my home?"

"I suppose. But when I think of a home, I think of someplace not so grand and definitely not so large. I mean, you could fit four, no, maybe eight or more of my apartment buildings inside the palace walls."

He shrugged. "I had nothing to do with its construction."

"But you don't mind living there—even though it's more like a museum than a home?"

He was quiet for a moment, as though giving her question due consideration. "I guess it's just what you are used to. I was born and raised here. For a long time, it was all I knew."

"And now that you've been out in the world, if you could choose something different for yourself, would you?" She knew it was a bold question to ask the crown prince, and maybe she should have refrained from asking it, but she was really curious about his answer.

"I don't know." His voice was so soft that she almost thought she'd dreamed it. But then he shifted in his seat and his gaze met hers. "I don't have the luxury of imagining a different life. My destiny was determined before I was born."

In that moment, she felt sorry for him, which was totally ridiculous. Why should she feel sorry for someone who had every imaginable luxury at his fingertips?

But there was this look in his eyes that tugged at her heartstrings. Before she could decipher its origins, he blinked and the look was gone.

In a soft tone, she said, "It's not fair. You should be able to choose your future."

He took her hand in his own. His thumb stroked the back of her hand, which did the craziest thing to her now-rapid pulse. "You're the first one to say something like that to me."

In that moment, she saw the man behind the title. He seemed so relatable. Because he wasn't the only one living a destiny that had been thrust upon him. She too was fulfilling the destiny left to her by her father—she was taking care of her mother by coming to this country, by facing the very people who had put her family on this painful course in life. But she didn't want to think of that now. It had no place in this magical evening.

As she gazed into Istvan's blue eyes, she was drawn to him. Neither of them had wanted these responsibilities, and yet neither of them could turn their backs on their families. In essence, they were trapped in their roles in life—his preparing to rule a kingdom, and her doing whatever it took to care for her mother.

His gaze dipped to her lips. Her heart *thump-*

thumped. His hold on her hand tightened. And then she felt her body leaning toward him.

Between the erratic heartbeats, reality got lost. The reasons that kissing him was a terribly bad idea were lost to her. The only thing she needed to know was what it was like to be in Istvan's embrace—to feel his lips upon hers. The breath lodged in her lungs as anticipation thrummed in her veins.

It felt as though time had slowed down and sped up all at once. One moment she was lounged back in her seat, and the next she was leaning over the center console into his strong, capable arms.

His warm lips pressed to hers. He didn't hesitate to deepen the kiss. His tongue traced her lips before delving past them. A moan emanated from him. It was though he needed this kiss as much as she did.

Her hand landed on his chest. She immediately appreciated the firm muscles beneath her fingertips. *Mighty fine. Mighty fine indeed.*

With the stars twinkling overhead, it was as though they were in their own little world. She didn't want this moment to end. When it did, she knew it would never happen again. And that made her all the more eager to make it last as long as possible. In fact, she wished this kiss would never end.

Her body tingled from head to foot. It'd been

a long time since she'd made out in a car. But it wasn't like this could happen in the palace, with so many people around from the staff to the queen hovering about. And definitely no one could know of this very special moment.

This stolen kiss would be both the beginning and the ending. Her heart squeezed with the bittersweetness of the situation. As the kiss deepened, she noticed that he tasted sweet, like the berries and champagne of their dessert. Her hand moved from his chest and wrapped around the back of his neck. Her fingertips combed through his thick hair, and a moan of delight swelled in the back of her throat.

They came from different worlds. He might not have directly banished her father, but assuming the role of crown prince meant he was willing to go along with his family's ruthless behavior.

She pulled back. *What am I doing? Being a traitor to Papa's memory.*

He blinked and looked at her. Confusion reflected in his eyes.

"That shouldn't have happened." She didn't wait for him to say anything as she yanked open the car door. She jumped out. She wasn't even sure she closed the door as she rushed across the parking lot.

"Indi, wait!"

She kept moving. She couldn't face him now. She had no idea what she'd say to him. The kiss had been mind-blowing, but it was so very wrong. As much fun as they undoubtedly could have together, it would lead to nothing but heartache when it was over.

She headed for the back of the palace. She just wanted to go home—her home. Her modest Greek apartment with her comfy bed and pillow, where she could hide away from the world, at least for the night.

But she wasn't afforded that luxury, as she had signed a contract to do this portrait.

She was let into the palace by one of the uniformed guards. Thankfully he recognized her. The last thing she wanted to do was have to explain her reason for being there—or worse, wait for Istvan to get her past security.

She rushed up the back stairway and prayed she wouldn't run into anyone. As luck would have it, when she reached the top of the stairs, she practically ran straight into the queen.

Indigo's heart launched into her throat. With effort, she swallowed. "Excuse me, ma'am. I didn't see you."

The queen's gaze narrowed. "Obviously. Do they not teach you manners where you come from?"

Indigo's shoulders straightened into a firm line. A smart retort teetered on the tip of her tongue. And then an image of her mother in her new apartment came to mind, and she swallowed down her indignation. Her mother had taught her that if she didn't have anything nice to say, sometimes it was best to say nothing at all. Though Indigo didn't necessarily subscribe to that way of thought, in this particular moment it was probably sage advice.

With gritted teeth, she did the slightest of curtsies. "Your Majesty."

The queen studied her as though making her mind up about her. "You know it won't work."

Indigo's heart rate accelerated. Did she know about them kissing? Impossible. They'd been hidden in the shadows of a tree. And somehow she didn't see the queen spending her time spying out windows. But that didn't stop the heat of embarrassment from blooming in her cheeks.

Not sure what the queen was referring to, she said, "Excuse me?"

"Trying to win over my son. You are a nobody—a wannabe. While he is royalty. He is the crown prince, and when he marries, it will be to someone of the finest upbringing with a grand lineage. He will not marry some commoner—some foreigner."

Indigo opened her mouth to protest the part about her being a foreigner. She was very much a Rydianian. But what good would that slight clarification do? And worse, it might make it seem like she was truly interested in Istvan, when nothing could be further from the truth. She pressed her lips together firmly.

Still, Indigo inwardly stewed about being called a foreigner. Both sides of her family had lived in Rydiania for many generations until the queen and king had abruptly forced her family from their home. The thought left a sour taste in the back of her mouth.

"Heed my warning. It's best you leave here. The sooner, the better." Then the queen snorted before lifting her chin and making her way in the opposite direction from Indigo's room.

Indigo's steps were quick and heavy as she made it to her room. How dare that woman look down her nose at her? At least she hadn't abandoned her family or forced them from the only home they'd known, like the royals had done to Istvan's uncle, King Georgios.

When she reached her room, Indigo stepped inside and let the door swing shut with a little more force than normal. In that moment, she didn't care if she made a scene. She was so over dealing with the royals.

If only she was over Istvan, too. The problem was the kiss had awakened a part of her that she hadn't known existed. It was the passionate part of her that was willing to suspend her rational thought in order to appease her desires—and she desired Istvan. A lot.

She flopped down on the huge four-poster bed

with a wine-colored comforter and about a hundred different-shaped pillows. Okay, maybe there weren't that many, but there were a lot.

Tap-tap.

"Indi, can we talk?"

Her heart thumped. Her initial instinct was to rush to the door and throw it open. She desperately wanted to see him again. But then what?

Would she throw herself into his arms? Or would she do the queen's bidding and warn him away? She was torn.

Tap-tap.

"Indi, please."

She needed time alone. And so, with great regret, she said, "Go away."

Her breath caught in her throat as she waited and listened. A moment of silence passed, and then the sound of his retreating footsteps could be heard.

What was she going to do? At this particular moment, she had no idea. She'd never expected to feel anything for the prince. And now that his kiss had awakened a bunch of emotions in her, she didn't know how to react.

What had he been thinking?

The truth was that he hadn't been thinking. Not at all.

He'd been acting out his desires. Ever since he'd spotted Indi at the Ludus Resort, he couldn't help but wonder what it'd be like to hold her in his arms and kiss her. And then once he'd gotten to know her better, his desire only grew.

Istvan sighed. Now that he'd given in to that driving desire, he'd royally messed things up. He clearly recalled the wide-eyed stare she'd given him after she'd pulled away from him. The memory tore at his gut. And then the way she'd fled from the car. She hadn't even stopped to close the door, that's how much she'd wanted to get away from him.

But why? That's the question he could not answer. No other woman had ever reacted that way after he'd kissed her. So what was so different about Indi?

His phone buzzed. He withdrew it from his pocket and found a testy message from the king's private secretary. Istvan was late for his meeting with the king, and his father was not happy.

With a groan of frustration, he made his way downstairs. Thoughts of Indi would have to wait until later. And then he would come up with a plan of how to fix things between them. Because surely there had to be a way to repair the damage that had been done. He just couldn't contemplate losing her friendship. She had brought a light to his life that he hadn't known he was missing. And without her, he feared being plunged back into the darkness.

He came to a stop outside his father's office.

He straightened his shirt, leaving the collar unbuttoned. Then he opened the door and stepped into the outer office of the king's secretary, who worked ridiculously long hours, just as his predecessors had done and those before them. The bald gentleman with gold wire-frame glasses glanced up from his computer monitor. The relief immediately showed in his eyes.

He briefly bowed his head. "The king is expecting you." He scurried to his feet. "Wait here." He disappeared inside the king's inner sanctum only to return a minute later. "The king will see you now."

Istvan was escorted into the king's office. "Your Majesty," the secretary said. "Prince Istvan has arrived."

The king nodded and then with his hand gestured for them to be left alone. The secretary backed out, never turning his back to the royals. And then the door softly snicked shut. They were alone.

"Your Majesty." Istvan bowed to his father as he'd been taught when he wasn't much more than a toddler.

His father was seated behind his desk. There was a mountain of papers on his desk. The king hadn't migrated to computers with the rest of the world and still preferred paper.

"Sit." The king's tone was terse.

Istvan moved to one of the two chairs in front

of the large oak desk. He knew he was in trouble, but that didn't bother him nearly as much as having Indi run away from him. He wondered what she was doing right now. So long as she wasn't packing to leave, he had a chance of fixing things. He hoped.

"You seem distracted," his father said. "I take it you've been spending your time with that woman."

"You mean Indigo. And yes, I took her to dinner in the village."

The king's brows rose. "Since when do we entertain the help?"

"She's not the help." The words came out faster than he'd intended. "Indigo is an artist that I've commissioned to do my formal portrait."

The king leaned back in his chair and steepled his fingers. "You've been away from the palace a lot lately. That needs to stop."

Istvan settled back in his chair. He refused to let his father think his disapproving tone or frown bothered him. In truth, Istvan didn't like being at odds with his parents, but they always assumed they were right and their decisions should be followed without question. The older Istvan got, the more their self-righteousness and immediate dismissal of his opinions grated on his nerves.

"I've been very busy on those trips." Istvan struggled to keep his rising temper at bay. "It's not like I was on vacation. I've been drumming up support for the We Care Foundation."

"That needs to stop."

Istvan couldn't believe his ears. "What must stop?"

"You will no longer work on that foundation."

"But I'm the one that founded it." He'd started it after little Jacques, a child from the village, came down with rare disease and his parents struggled to keep their jobs and spend time at the hospital. Istvan had felt the need to do something to help families in similar circumstances.

"Give it to one of your aides. Or better yet, let the staff of the foundation handle it."

Istvan's fingers tightened on the arms of the chair. "That won't be happening."

The king's brows knitted together, creating a formidable line. "You're refusing?"

Istvan sat up straight. "This project is personal to me, and I intend to continue overseeing it. Now, if there's nothing else—"

"There is one other matter. The woman you brought here. She needs to go."

Istvan's anger bubbled to the surface. "The woman has a name. It's Indigo. And she's not leaving until she's fulfilled her contract."

"Istvan, I don't know what's gotten into you, but this is unacceptable. When your king gives you an order, you are to follow it without question."

"When my king's requests are more reasonable, I will take them into consideration." And with that he got to his feet. He gave a brief bow of his head, and then he turned. With his shoulders ramrod straight, he strode to the door.

He couldn't get out of the office fast enough. He was afraid if he stayed he would say something he would regret. And that wouldn't have done his foundation a bit of good. Because whether Istvan liked it or not, the king had the power to shut it down. That thought didn't sit well with Istvan.

When he was young, he'd believed everything he was told—that the king and queen always knew what was best, that the king and queen had been placed at the head of the kingdom by God, and that everyone should follow the direction of the king and queen without question.

But then his beloved uncle, who had been king, stepped down from the throne. Istvan had never understood his uncle's choice to give up the crown. After all, if you were chosen by God for such a mighty position, how could you possibly walk away from it?

And then there were the actions of his father after he'd become the new king. He'd banished his own flesh-and-blood brother from the kingdom. By royal decree, Istvan's uncle could never step foot on Rydianian soil again. And it was not only his uncle but his uncle's Immediate staff. They were all cast out of the realm.

For a six-year-old, it was a lot to take in. Istvan hadn't seen the crown quite the same way after losing his favorite uncle. And when he was forbidden to make contact with Uncle Georgios, Istvan had promised himself that he would track down his uncle as soon as he was old enough to travel alone.

It hadn't been until he was eighteen that he was able to escape his security team and travel to the Ludus Resort, where he was reunited with his uncle and he met his uncle's wife. It had been awkward at first as he'd had many questions for his uncle about the past—a past that his uncle hadn't been so willing to discuss.

The closer Istvan got to assuming the crown, the more he wanted to make changes. He knew his parents would be horrified. In fact, if the king and queen knew he envisioned more of a democracy for the kingdom, they wouldn't step aside and let him take over. Of that he was certain.

And the other thing he was certain of was that Indigo wasn't going anywhere until his portrait was completed. She had a contract, and if it came to it, he intended to enforce it. He just hoped it didn't come to that.

CHAPTER TWELVE

OH, WHAT A KISS.

Indigo yawned again. And again. She'd tossed and turned for a large portion of the night. Even her morning shower hadn't wakened her the way it normally did.

Countless times she'd replayed the kiss with Istvan. And though she wanted to put all the blame on him, she couldn't do it. She'd wanted to kiss him, too. She'd tried to remember who'd made the first move. Or had they moved at the same time?

She supposed it didn't matter now. The kiss was an undeniable thing between them. And she had no idea how to deal with it. Did they talk it out? Did she explain why it couldn't happen again? Or did she pretend it had never happened? Like that was possible.

During the wee hours of the morning, she'd recalled the Ruby Heart and the folklore about how lovers viewing it together would be forever linked or some such thing. Last night, she'd let herself believe some sort of spell had been cast over them and that's why they'd given in to their desires. But in the light of day, she realized how ridiculous it sounded and reminded herself that she didn't believe in folklore or legends.

Showered and dressed, she glanced in the mirror. She'd put on a little more makeup today than she normally would have in order to hide the shadows under her eyes. And there was her hair…should she wear it up? Or down?

This was her third day in Rydiania. It was time to get to work. She glanced at the antique clock. It was seven-thirty. She had to hurry. She wanted to arrive early for the prince's first sitting so she could set up for the portrait. And then she'd have a private word with Istvan about why they needed to pretend the kiss had never happened.

She grabbed her supplies and headed for the door. The problem was that she had no idea where she was headed. She had to stop and ask someone, who had to make an inquiry of someone else, before she was directed to a vast room. The only piece of furniture in the entire room was a single wing-back chair. She couldn't tell if the room was always devoid of furniture or if it had been cleared for the portrait.

The room was too small for a ballroom and yet too large to be a sitting room. But the exterior wall was nothing but big windows. The other three walls were done with white wainscoting on the bottom, while the upper walls were done in a cool brown tone. Sconces were spaced throughout, with various framed nature photos showing the seasons from winter to autumn.

And then she realized where she was—the conservatory. She hadn't immediately recognized it with it being devoid of furnishings. It was such a beautiful room. If this was her home, she'd turn this room into her studio, as it was filled with natural light.

She positioned the chair closer to the windows. She wanted to be able to pick up every nuance of Istvan's handsome face. She knew no matter how long she lived that she would never forget him or the kiss they'd shared. But she couldn't let it distract her. She was here to do a job—a job that would secure her mother's care and independence.

And that was the reason she'd decided to act as though the kiss hadn't happened. It was the only way they were going to move beyond it. She could do this. She could act like that kiss hadn't rocked her world.

"Good morning."

She immediately recognized Istvan's deep voice. She swallowed hard, straightened her shoulders and turned. She forced a smile to her lips. "Morning."

"I stopped by your room and was surprised to find that you were gone already."

"I wanted to get here early and set up. I know you don't have much time, with your guests arriving today. This is a wonderful room to work in. The large windows are perfect. And I hope you don't mind that I moved the chair. I mean, I could put it back, but I thought the lighting was better over here." She pressed her lips together to stop her rambling.

Istvan stepped up to her. "It's fine. Whatever setup you want works for me. But is that really what you have on your mind?"

Her gaze moved to his. Her heart pounded in her chest. *Just pretend the kiss didn't happen.* "I... I think it would be best if we focus on the portrait and nothing else."

Istvan didn't say anything for a moment. "So you just want to act like last night never happened?"

"Yes." She kept her arms at her sides, resisting the urge to wring her hands.

"Are you sure you can resist the temptation?" He arched a dark brow.

What was he trying to say? Did that kiss mean more to him than a passing flirtation? Of course not. After all, he was a prince. And she was, what? An artist. She certainly wasn't fit to be his...what? Girlfriend? Nervous laughter bubbled up inside her. She quickly stifled it.

"I can resist." Two could play at this game. "But can you?"

"I'm not making any promises."

She narrowed her gaze. "If you want me to complete this portrait, you can't be distracting me."

He planted his hands on his trim waist. "Did you just call me a distraction?"

"You know what they say…if the shoe fits."

She couldn't tell if he was flirting with her or just having fun. Perhaps it was a bit of both. Whichever, it was still better than the tension of last night. The flirting she could handle. It was the kissing that totally tripped her up.

He smiled and shook his head. "Are you ready to get started?"

She glanced around at the armchair and her easel. Suddenly this setting just didn't feel right, at least not to get started. "How about I just follow you around today? You know, while you're working or whatever."

"Who am I to argue? I've got a lot to catch up on from when I was on Ludus Island."

"Then lead the way and I shall follow."

He arched a brow. "You're sure about this? Because I have to warn you that it'll get boring."

"Don't worry about me. Just act like I'm not there."

"That would be impossible." He sent her a warm smile that caused a flutter in her chest. "But I shall do my best."

She grabbed her bag with her supplies and slung it over her shoulder. On their way out the door, they passed an older gentleman with white hair. He was dressed in a dark suit, and he had an easel in one hand. Another artist?

Her gaze moved between the two men. They seemed to know each other. Her curiosity was piqued. Was this man her replacement? She hadn't even done her first sketch and she was already being let go.

She recalled the queen's insistence that the palace's artist would do the prince's portrait. Indigo had thought Istvan would stand up to his mother and tell her what he wanted, but it appeared that once more the crown had won out.

Inside, Indigo was totally crushed. She hadn't known until that moment how much she'd been looking forward to completing such an important project. She could hang her entire artistic future on this one assignment. And now it was about to end before it even began.

"Your Highness." The man bowed. When he straightened, he said, "I am here to work on your portrait."

She caught the older man staring at her. Disapproval showed in his eyes as he took in her white-and-yellow summer top paired with jeans. Then he lifted his nose ever so slightly and turned his attention back to the prince.

What was it with this man to turn up his nose to her? Her body stiffened as angry words clogged her throat. She'd had just about enough of everyone in this palace thinking they were better than her. Not even the prince had treated her so disrespectfully.

Although the prince had apparently caved in to his mother's wishes, and now she was out of a job. Her jaw tightened as she resisted throwing accusations at the prince in front of an audience. Why would he continue to string her along?

"I won't be sitting for the portrait today." Istvan's voice drew her attention. "I have business that requires my attention."

The older man momentarily frowned but quickly hid his reaction. "Yes, Your Highness."

After they'd moved some distance down the hallway for some privacy, she stopped walking. "What's going on?"

Istvan paused and turned to her. He wore a sheepish expression. "I may have forgotten to mention that I am having two portraits done."

She frowned at him. "If you no longer wanted my services, all you had to do was say so."

He shook his head. "It isn't that. I still want you to do my portrait."

She crossed her arms. "Why, when you already have the palace's artist doing one?"

He stepped closer to her. She took a step back. He sighed as he raked his fingers through his hair. "You don't understand what it's like with my parents. When they want something, they don't stop until they get it."

"Why keep me here when you know you'll end up using the other portrait?"

"That's not my intention. But in the meantime, it's easier to appease my mother."

Indigo didn't like what she was hearing. Istvan was giving in to his parents. And to her way of thinking, that meant he condoned their decisions. The thought left a bitter taste in the back of her mouth.

If she'd had any second thoughts about abruptly ending their kiss, she no longer did. She couldn't trust Istvan. He was one of them—no matter how much she wished he was different. He was the prince of Rydiania, now and always.

CHAPTER THIRTEEN

A WEEK HAD passed since she'd arrived at the palace. The last several days, the royal family had hosted the country's business leaders, leaving very little time for Indigo to observe the prince.

She'd resorted to taking photos of him. She promised herself that she would delete them as soon as the portrait was complete. She would not keep them and stare at them, wondering what might have been had they met under different circumstances.

And now the moment she'd been dreading had arrived. Dinner with the family.

When Istvan had mentioned it, he'd made it sound so normal. Indigo knew having a meal with his family was anything but normal. Her stomach shivered with nerves.

She wished they could slip away to dine in the village again. The small town was so laid-back and the people so welcoming. It was everything the palace wasn't—warm and inviting. But then again, their dinner in the village had ended with them kissing, so maybe that wasn't such a good idea.

She felt as though she were going to dine with the enemies. How could two people who were so cold as to cast out their own relative, not to mention his loyal staff, have a son who was so friendly and seemingly caring for others?

Indigo sighed as she stared at her selection of dresses. She didn't know which to choose. Istvan had said not to worry, that it was going to be a casual family dinner. She glanced down at her jeans and cotton top. Definitely too casual.

Knock-knock.

"Come in." She expected it to be Istvan checking in on her.

When the door opened, a young maid appeared. Indigo had met her before, but for the life of her, she couldn't remember her name. "Hi."

The young woman smiled. "I am here to see if I can help you prepare for dinner."

"Help me?" she mumbled to herself. Suddenly she worried that she'd totally misunderstood this dinner. Perhaps she needed a few more details. "Uh, come in and close the door."

The young woman did so. "How may I help you?"

It was best to get the awkward part over with first. "I'm so sorry, but I can't recall your name."

"It's Alice, ma'am."

"Please, call me Indigo."

"Yes, ma'am... I mean Indigo. How can I help you?"

"I'm not sure what to wear to dinner. The prince said it will be casual, but I'm not sure which dress to wear." She held out her top two choices from the wardrobe. One was a white summer dress and the other was a little black dress that could be accessorized to make it fancier.

The maid eyed both choices. Her expression was devoid of emotion, leaving Indigo at a loss as to what Alice was thinking.

"May I suggest something else?" Alice asked.

Indigo could use all the help she could get so she didn't embarrass herself in front of the royal family. Not that she was trying to impress them, because what they thought didn't mean a thing to her. But what Istvan thought was starting to matter to her. She didn't want to do anything to ruin this evening for him.

"Yes, please." She couldn't help but wonder what Alice had in mind.

"I'll be right back." Alice disappeared out the door.

Indigo hung up the dresses. She felt so out of place here, where casual wasn't even casual. She wondered if it was too late to plead a headache again. At this rate, it wouldn't be a lie.

This was not going to go well.

Istvan had had a sinking feeling in his gut ever

since his mother had insisted on a family dinner that evening—including Indi. He'd warned his mother to be on her best behavior where Indi was concerned. His mother didn't take well to warnings, but he wasn't about to have her drive Indi away.

When the king had overheard the conversation, he'd told Istvan that he was overreacting. After all, it was a family dinner, not an inquisition. Istvan wished he had a normal family and not one that was constantly worried about protecting their public image.

Istvan stepped in front of the mirror to check his tie. He adjusted it just a little. Then he buttoned the top button on his suit jacket and headed for the door. He hoped Indigo was ready. Being late to dinner wouldn't go over well with his very punctual parents. Though his youngest sister was notorious for being late.

He wanted this first meal with his family and Indigo to go well. As much as he didn't want to admit that his parents' opinions mattered to him, they still did. And if they just gave Indigo a chance, he was certain they would see there was something special about her.

He made his way to Indi's door and knocked. "Come in."

He opened the door and stepped inside. When he caught sight of Indi, her back was to him. It appeared she was struggling with the zipper on her dress.

He paused to take in her beauty—some of her hair was pulled up and held with sparkly pins while the rest fell past her shoulders in long, elegant curls.

"You're just in time. I need help with this zipper."

His gaze lowered to the smooth skin of her back. His pulse picked up. He moved across the room. He reached for the zipper and gave it a tug. It didn't move.

"I think it's caught on some material."

Before he could work on loosening the zipper, she spun around. Her eyes were wide with surprise. "I thought you were Alice."

"Sorry to surprise you." He waited, wondering if she would send him away.

Her gaze moved to the closed doorway and then back to him. "I don't want to be late for dinner." She turned back around. "Do you think you can fix the zipper?"

"I can try." He had to admit that most of his experience was with lowering zippers, not pulling them up.

When his fingertips brushed over her smooth skin, it sent his heart racing. He tugged at the zipper. It refused to move.

His gaze strayed to the nape of her neck. If he were to lean forward and press his lips to that one particular spot, he wondered what sort of response it would elicit from her. The idea was so tempting that he couldn't resist. He leaned closer.

"Is it broken?" Indigo spun around.

His face was only a couple of centimeters from hers. The breath hitched in his throat. His gaze caught and held hers. He noticed how she didn't back away. In fact, she didn't move as she continued to stare at him with desire evident in her eyes.

His gaze dipped to her glossy lips. They were oh, so tempting. And then his vision lowered to the place on her neck that pulsated. That was where he would start. *Oh, yes.*

His hands reached out, gripping her rounded hips. He lowered his head slowly. She didn't move. He inhaled the sweet scent of primrose that reminded him of a cool spring evening with a bit of tangy, fruity sort of twist that was mingled with the hint of vanilla. Mmm...what a heady combination.

When his lips touched her smooth skin, he heard a distinct hiss as she sucked in air. Her pulse beat wildly under his lips. Her heart wasn't the only one beating wildly.

He began kissing his way up her neck to her jaw. It was slow and deliciously agonizing. He couldn't wait to pull her close and claim her lips beneath his. And if that little moan he heard in Indi's throat was any indication, she was enjoying this moment as much as he was.

Knock-knock.

He heard the click of the doorknob and the slight squeak of the door hinge. A gasp sounded behind him.

With the greatest regret, Istvan pulled away from Indi. As he drew in a deep, calming breath, his gaze strayed across her mouth. Frustration knotted up his gut.

With great restraint, he placed a pleasant look on his face and turned to find the maid with pink-stained cheeks.

"I'm so sorry," Alice said. "I should go."

"No. Please stay," Indigo said. All the while she avoided looking at Istvan. "The zipper on my dress is stuck and, um…the prince was trying to free it, but it won't budge."

So that's what he was doing? He smiled. Just then Indigo's gaze met his, and he let out a laugh. She might be ready to deny the chemistry sizzling between them, but he knew the truth. And this wasn't the end. It was merely a pause—to be continued later.

Had that really happened?

Had she been kissed by the prince? Again?

Indigo's heart raced every time she recalled his hot breath on her neck and the delicious sensations he'd sent cascading throughout her body. If they hadn't been interrupted, she wondered just how far things would have gone.

When his lips had pressed to her skin, reality had spiraled out of reach. All she could think about was how amazing he'd made her feel and how much she wanted more—so much more.

But that couldn't happen. His future was here in Rydiania, and she shouldn't be here. The truth was they were never, ever supposed to mean anything to each other.

Going forward, she couldn't let her guard down around him. The prince didn't seem to mind playing with fire, but she for one didn't intend to get burned. She'd already lost enough in this lifetime. She wasn't about to lose any more—including her heart.

With her zipper fixed, she was ready for dinner. She stepped out into the hallway, where Istvan was waiting for her. This was the first time she was able to take in his appearance, in a navy-blue suit and white dress shirt with a boring blue tie. Her imagination stripped away the proper shirt and tie to reveal his tanned chest. As soon as the thought came to her, she halted it.

Her mouth grew dry, and she swallowed hard. "I'm ready… I think."

He sent her a slow smile that lifted his mouth ever so slightly at the corners. "Don't worry. This is just a casual family dinner. And if you need further assistance with your zipper, I'm available."

"Istvan, stop." Heat flamed in her cheeks.

"I'm just offering to help."

"Thanks, but no. You've helped quite enough. The whole palace staff is going to think we're having some wild affair."

He gazed into her eyes. "And would that be so bad?"

"No. I mean, yes." She exhaled a frustrated sigh. It was best to change the subject. "You said this dinner was to be casual, but my understanding of casual doesn't include formal attire."

"Ah…but see, that's where you're wrong. This is formal casual. Formal attire would be a tux and a gown."

"Sorry. I'm not up on my royal fashion trends."

"Then stick with me. I'll show you how it's done." He presented his arm to her.

She hesitated, but at the moment her legs felt a bit wobbly. The last thing she needed to do was to take a tumble down that long flight of stairs. And after all, it was just a hand in the crook of his arm. It wasn't like having his lips pressed to the sensitive part of her neck.

In that moment, her gaze dipped to his mouth—oh, that amazing mouth. She wondered at all the wonderful things he could do with it. Not that she would ever know, but it didn't keep her from wondering.

"That will have to wait until later." His voice drew her from her errant thoughts.

She lifted her gaze to meet his. She'd been

busted daydreaming. Heat rushed to her cheeks and made them burn. She should glance away, but she didn't.

She leveled her shoulders and tilted her chin upward ever so slightly. "That will never happen again."

"You said that before, and yet look at what just happened." He led them toward the grand staircase.

"That was your fault."

"I didn't hear any complaints. I wonder what would happen if I were to kiss you right here and now."

She stopped and yanked her hand free. "Don't you dare."

"Oh, but I would dare." His eyes twinkled with mischief.

"If you think I can't resist you just because you're a handsome prince, think again." *Wait.* Did she just admit that she thought he was handsome? Inwardly she cringed, but outwardly she refused to acknowledge her faux pas.

"As much as I'd like to continue this debate with you, we can't be late for dinner."

She was relieved to put an end to this awkward conversation. "Agreed."

"Shall we?" He once more held his arm out to her.

This time she accepted his gesture. She refused to acknowledge the way being so close to him made her heart beat out of control. *Nope. Not going there.*

She couldn't remember where the private dining room was in the palace. There were just so many rooms that it could easily be converted into a high-end hotel. Not that Istvan would ever consider it. Still, it was so big just to be a private residence. She couldn't imagine ever calling this place her home.

As they made their way down the grand staircase, she imagined the foyer filled with formally dressed partygoers. Okay. So living here might have its benefits. The parties must be out of this world. Not that she would ever get to attend one with Istvan.

Her gaze moved to him. Her heart pitter-pattered. He was certainly the sexiest date—*erm, escort*—she'd ever had. And there was a part of her that was really curious to know how far things would have gone if they hadn't been interrupted. She quelled a sigh.

Once on the main floor, he guided her to a hallway that led toward the back of the palace. Their footsteps were muffled by a long red runner. The halls were so wide that it felt strange for her to refer to them as hallways. They were like huge, long rooms with a lot of closed doors to each side. And in between were couches—the kind you'd be afraid to sit on, because they looked like pieces of art. In addition, there were ornate pieces of furniture as well as priceless statues and large ceramic vases.

"Something catch your interest?" he asked.

She shook her head. "I'm just taking it all in."

"There's a lot to take in." That was an understatement.

He stopped in front of a set of double doors and turned to her. "Are you ready for this?"

Her heart started to pound. Her palms grew damp. And her mouth grew dry. This would be her first time meeting the king—the man ultimately responsible for the demise of her father. That thought ignited an old flame of anger. She would not let him intimidate her.

Every muscle in her body tensed as she turned to Istvan. "Let's do this."

He sent her a reassuring smile. "Let's."

Istvan grabbed both of the gold door handles. He swung both of the doors wide-open. Her heart leaped into her throat. She felt as though she were walking into the lion's den.

On wooden legs, she passed by Istvan and entered the room. She was pretty certain she was supposed to follow him, with him being a prince, but, ever the gentleman, he let her go first. Although she wasn't sure he'd done her any favors as every head turned in her direction.

Silence fell over the room. Her fingernails dug into her palms. *You can do this. You can do this.* She continued to repeat the mantra.

The king looked like an older version of Istvan, with gray temples and a close-trimmed beard that was peppered with gray. The man didn't smile. His gaze seemed to study her. All the while her insides shivered with nerves. What was he thinking? Did he see a resemblance to her father? Impossible. Everyone said she favored her mother.

"Father," Istvan said, "this is Indigo. She's a remarkable artist, and I've invited her to the palace to do my portrait."

The king's intense gaze never moved from her, though when he spoke it was in reply to his son. "I'm not used to you bringing the hired help to the dinner table."

"Indigo isn't hired help. She's a talented artist and my friend."

Indigo's back teeth ground together. Would it be wrong to tell the king what she thought of him? Probably. And it would definitely have her out of a job. The thought of what this job meant to her mother's quality of life was the only thing that kept her quiet.

She continued to hold the king's gaze. If he thought she was going to glance away or bow, he had another thought coming. There was only so far she would go to keep this job.

"Welcome." The king's voice lacked any warmth.

She couldn't tell if he was always cold or if it was just her presence that brought out his frosty side. "Your Majesty."

"Let's get you seated," Istvan said.

When her gaze surveyed the table, she found two available seats. They were not side by side, like she'd been hoping. Instead they were at opposite ends of the table. One was by the king. The other was next to the queen. Indigo groaned inwardly. Why exactly had she agreed to this dinner?

"She can sit down here," the queen said.

And so the decision was taken out of her hands. All the while the three princesses watched the scene unfold. Whatever their thoughts about the situation, they weren't revealed on their faces. Indigo wondered if that blank stare was something taught or if it was inherited.

Her stomach was tied in a knot as she took a seat to the queen's left while Istvan took a seat to the king's left. At least she could glance in Istvan's direction now and then. But the table was so long that trying to make any conversation with him was nearly impossible unless she wanted to yell.

The meal was slow, and the timings appeared to depend on when the king finished each course. When he was done, the table was cleared, whether others were done or not. Indigo didn't figure this out until the third course. Needless to say, she didn't finish the first two courses.

Conversation was sparse around the table. She

wondered if the silence was due to her presence or if it was always this quiet.

At last, the queen asked, "So how exactly did you present yourself to my son?"

Was the queen even speaking normal English? "I didn't *present* myself to him." Was it so beyond the queen's thinking to imagine her son might seek out female company all on his own? "He stopped by my umbrella for a sketch."

Twin lines formed between the queen's brows. "An umbrella?"

Indigo went on to explain her position at the Ludus Resort. The queen listened, as did the princesses, but the men were involved in their own conversation. Each time she glanced in Istvan's direction, he appeared absorbed in his discussion with his father.

"My son wanted you to draw a cartoon of him?" Disapproval rang out in the queen's tone.

"It's a caricature. And it's not exactly a cartoon. It's an exaggerated drawing."

"I don't understand why he'd want you to do his portrait. This portrait is very important. It can't be a cartoon. Thank goodness I've had the forethought to schedule the palace's portrait artist."

Indigo's pride bristled at the queen's disdain over her artistic skills—skills the woman hadn't even witnessed. "I've studied art my whole life.

I grew up with a paintbrush in my hand. I am capable of much more than caricatures."

"So your family is in Greece?" the queen asked, dismissing what Indigo had just said.

"Yes. My mother is there."

"It's just the two of you?" When Indigo nodded, the queen said, "Then you must be anxious to return."

"Actually, I am. I have…" She hesitated. She didn't want to share her gallery showing with the queen just to have her make a snide comment about it. "…a job to return to."

"I understand. That sounds important. I'll see that you are on the next flight back to Greece."

Wow! Talk about a bold brush-off. But the queen wasn't the first difficult person she'd had to deal with. And she wasn't going to be rushed off. Not a chance.

"Thank you, but my job here isn't complete yet." She placed her fork on the table. Her appetite was long gone. "Please excuse me. I have some phone calls to make."

There was a gasp from one of the princesses as Indigo got to her feet. With her head held high, she moved toward the door, skirting around the waitstaff as they carried in the main course. She didn't dare look at Istvan. She didn't want to see the disapproval on his face. He should just be happy that she hadn't said what she was really thinking.

She kept putting one foot in front of the other. This assignment wouldn't be over soon enough. She couldn't wait to get out of this kingdom— away from these people.

She was almost to the stairs when she heard her name being called out. It was Istvan's voice. She didn't slow down. She didn't want to talk to him right now.

He must have jogged to catch up with her, because the next thing she knew, his hand was on her arm. "Indi, wait."

She stopped at the bottom of the steps and turned to him. "I know you want me to apologize, but I'm not sorry. Your mother... She's..." She groaned in frustration.

"I know. And I'm the one who's sorry. I thought my parents would act better than that." He rubbed his neck. "I didn't mean to make you so uncomfortable. Let me make it up to you."

She shook her head. "I'm just going to call it a night."

"But you haven't had much to eat."

"I'm not hungry. Good night."

She continued up the steps. She could feel Istvan's gaze upon her, but he let her go. She wasn't good company tonight. She needed to call home and remind herself why she was staying here when all she wanted to do was leave.

CHAPTER FOURTEEN

THINGS WERE NOT going well.

Sure, his meetings that morning had been productive. And he was starting to catch up on the work that had piled up while he'd been away on Ludus Island, but it was Indi that had him worried.

Ever since she'd found out that he was having two portraits done, she had been unusually quiet and her sunny smile was missing. It was though a big, dark cloud was hovering over them. And last night's disaster of a dinner hadn't helped matters.

He was quickly finding that he never quite knew where he stood with Indi. One moment everything was fine. They would be laughing and talking. The next moment she was looking at him like he was the enemy. He just wanted to find some common ground where they could begin to trust each other.

As his meeting with his secretary about next month's calendar concluded, he could see that Indi was utterly bored. He'd even caught her hiding a yawn not once but twice. It was time for a new plan.

"I'm sorry that took so long," he said.

She waved off his comment. "No problem. I got a lot done."

He'd seen her pencil move over her sketch pad throughout his meetings. He was very curious to see what she'd been up to. "May I see?"

She clutched her sketch pad to her chest. "No one sees a work in progress."

"But that isn't even the portrait."

"It's the groundwork. You'll have to use some patience."

Throughout his meetings, he'd been distracted by Indi's presence. He'd worked hard to hide his interest in her, but he couldn't hide it from himself. He became quite impatient—to make her smile, to hear her laughter, to feel her lips pressed to his. He jerked his errant thoughts to a complete halt.

What was he doing? There had never been anyone in his life who could utterly distract him. And yet somehow Indi had gotten past his carefully laid defenses to make him care about her. The revelation stilled the air in his lungs.

That wasn't possible. He was just overthinking things. He had to be careful, because with him being the crown prince, he didn't have the liberty to get involved with just anyone. When he got serious about a woman, she had to be the right woman. How many times had his parents told him that?

His future queen had to come with the right background. She had to be perfectly cultured, beautiful and submissive to the authority of the crown.

Though Indi was the most beautiful woman he'd ever known, she was most definitely not submissive—far from it. She had a mind of her own, and she wasn't afraid to speak her opinion—though she did pick and choose the times she shared what she was thinking.

Enough. He needed a distraction. In fact, perhaps it was time for them to go to lunch. He was thinking of heading into the village and perhaps taking time for a visit to the art gallery. He was certain that would return the smile to her face. He grabbed his phone and texted his secretary to arrange a showing at the gallery that afternoon.

Even if they couldn't have anything more between them than what they had today, it didn't mean they couldn't be good friends—genuine friends. He had enough people in his life that told him what they thought he wanted to hear. Indi didn't do that. She told him the truth whether he liked it or not. He needed her in his life. She grounded him.

With the meeting concluded, he checked his phone and found the answer he wanted from the gallery. He got to his feet and rounded the desk.

"I have to meet someone in the village. Would you care to join me?"

Her eyes lit up for the first time that day. "I would like that. Would you mind if I made a detour to the art gallery?"

"Not at all. I actually had that in mind, too." He smiled at her.

She didn't smile back. "Let me just grab my purse from my room."

"I'll meet you out on the drive."

And then she was gone. She might not have smiled yet, but he was certain she wouldn't be able to refrain when they got to the gallery. He grabbed his phone and made a call to confirm that they were on their way. Hopefully it'd get him back on Indi's good side.

Excitement flooded her veins.

This village was where she was born—where her father and mother were born. She never thought she would see this place in person. And now she was here walking through her past—a past she'd been too young to remember.

Still, she felt as though she were at last at home. She knew that wasn't the case, but it just felt like…well, like she belonged. And she would have if it hadn't been for Istvan's family. She'd still have her father, and perhaps her mother's health wouldn't have failed.

She gave herself a mental shake. Instead she

focused on her memories. After they'd moved to Greece, her father used to tell her about the village. She strove to recall those stories.

Her father would talk about a fountain in a small square. She wondered if she could find it. "I love the village. Are there any piazzas?"

"There's a town square not far from here."

Excitement pumped through her veins. "Does it by chance have a fountain?"

"It does. Would you like to see it?"

She nodded. "I would. I love exploring old towns."

In a few minutes they were in the old town square. There were a few two-story buildings on each side. They were all colorfully painted. And the second stories had small balconies. She couldn't help but wonder if these were the original colors. If so, she might be able to find the exact building where she was born.

"I just love the colors. Were they always this color?" She tried to sound casual as her gaze took in the older buildings that held so much character.

"I think so. At least as far back as I can remember."

This made it easy for her. She moved to stand next to the fountain. Her gaze took in the sidewalk café, the bakery whose buttery scent made her mouth water and the florist with bright, colorful blooms filling the big picture window. And then her gaze landed on an indigo-blue building.

Her gaze lifted to the small white balcony and the windows of the second floor. That had been her parents' home. It was the place where she'd taken her first breath.

A rush of emotion came over her. She blinked repeatedly. She had to keep it together in front of Istvan. She didn't want him to know that this place—this country—meant anything to her. She wouldn't give him or his family that power over her.

"Indi, did you hear me?"

She blinked and turned to him. "What did you say?"

"I asked if you want to have lunch here?"

"Yes. I'd like that."

And so they made their way to the cute outdoor café. She remained quiet as she was overcome by so many emotions from seeing her home to standing next to the sexiest man that she'd ever known. When he looked at her, it was like he could see straight through her. And then there was the way her heart pitter-pattered every time he smiled at her.

As they waited for their meals, she said, "I love it here."

"I do, too. I learn a lot from the villagers."

"What sorts of things do you learn?"

"That the village needs a children's after-school program."

"And is that something you're interested in starting?"

"It is." He toyed with a red swizzle stick resting on the white tablecloth. "I've already set up a children's foundation. It provides free accommodations for the parents of sick children and also provides a modest allowance to help with lost wages while their child is sick."

She was stunned into silence. *Wow!* There really was another side to him. And she was mighty impressed. "Your parents must be so proud of you."

"Not exactly. My parents and I have different views of what my responsibilities should be as the crown prince. They want me to do things the way they've always been done."

"And what do you want to do?"

"I want to change things. I think change is vital to the survival of the royal family. And more importantly, I think change is vital to Rydiania. Without keeping up with the changing times and investing in technology, we will fall very far behind the other European countries."

"And while you are worrying about all that, you're running a foundation to help sick children and their parents?"

He nodded. "A three-year-old from the village became very sick. Treatment was in the city. With the parents being there for their son, they weren't able to keep up with their jobs, and they eventually lost everything. I didn't know about it until after they'd lost their jobs and home."

"Talk about making a tough time even worse."

"Agreed. So the foundation is also promoting job protection while caring for a sick family member, but the king won't make it law, because it will change the way things have always been done. When I am king, it's one of the first things I plan to do, whether my parents agree or not. I guess I'm more like my uncle than anyone ever realized."

And then their food was delivered to the table, which was a shame, because she wanted to know what his last comment meant. She suspected he was referring to the uncle who had abdicated the throne. Was Istvan thinking of abdicating, too?

Just as quick as the ridiculous thought came to her, she dismissed it. First of all, he didn't have a throne to abdicate. He was still the crown prince. And he had all these wonderful plans for the country. A person who was thinking of walking away from the crown wouldn't be making plans.

Still, the more she learned about the prince, the more intrigued she became. Something told her if it was up to him, his uncle wouldn't have been cast out of kingdom, along with his most trusted staff and their families.

CHAPTER FIFTEEN

LUNCH FOR TWO at an outdoor café.

The delicious meal had done the trick.

When Indigo smiled, Istvan relaxed. At last things between them were good once more. And he wanted it to stay that way. They only had four days left together. It didn't seem nearly long enough.

With the bill paid, they headed on their way. He made a quick stop by the bank to discuss some foundation business. Indigo opted to wait outside. She seemed to have fallen in love with the village. He had to admit that it was quaint but held its own unique charms.

His business didn't take long. When he exited the bank, he found Indigo sitting on a nearby bench. She had a book in her hands and was so captivated by the words on the page that she didn't hear him approach.

He cleared his throat. When she glanced up at him, she had a distant look in her eyes. He smiled. "Did you find something interesting?"

"I did." She gathered her things and stood. She turned the cover of the book so he could read it. "I've been reading about the history of this village. It has quite an illustrious history, from wars to royalty."

"So you like it here?"

"If you mean this village, I love it."

"Me, too."

He'd never felt such a closeness with anyone—even when Indi was miffed with him. But he had a surprise for her that he was hoping would make up for the earlier upset.

"Are you ready for your gallery tour?" he asked as they began to walk.

"I am." She smiled brightly at him.

They walked in a peaceful silence. Each of them was lost in their own thoughts. He was thinking about how much it had bothered him when Indigo believed he'd broken his word to her. He'd felt horrible about the misunderstanding.

And if he had been that bothered by her being upset with him, how was he going to cope when she flew back to Greece on Friday? He wanted to ask her to stay longer, but how long would be enough?

His thoughts halted when they reached the big white building that was home to the Belle Galleria. "We have arrived."

"I can't wait." A bright smile lit up her face.

Then her gaze moved to the glass door, and the smile slipped from her face.

"What's wrong?"

"The gallery's closed today."

"Don't worry. We're having a private showing."

Her eyes widened. "You arranged this?"

He nodded. "I did. I know how important it is to you."

"Thank you. But you shouldn't have." Her gaze lowered. "I feel awful that people had to come in on their day off."

He could tell she wasn't used to people making a fuss over her. "It's all right. I made sure they were adequately compensated."

Just then someone approached the doors. They unlocked them and pushed them open. As Indi stepped inside, he thought of the other surprise he had in store for her.

The gallery was painted white with a slate-gray floor. The walls were covered in canvases, while vitrines were strategically placed throughout the large room. Within the lighted glass cases were smaller artistic pieces. Some were pieces of jewelry, and others were delicate structures constructed of wire or wood.

Istvan had visited the gallery many times. He found it peaceful and relaxing. And so he followed Indi around, letting her set the pace. She was unusually quiet as she took time to study each piece of work. He wanted to know what she was thinking, but he didn't want to interrupt her process. He was content just to watch her quietly.

Every now and then she'd make a comment. He listened and observed. By touring the gallery with Indi, he was able to see the art with a totally new appreciation.

And then she came to a stop. He almost ran into her.

She gasped. "It's mine."

He didn't have to look to know what she'd stumbled across. This was his other surprise. "I wanted to share your caricature with others."

Her eyes were filled with confusion. "I thought you wanted to auction it off."

"Ah…yes. I still plan to do that with the second sketch. But this is the first sketch you did for me. After I had it framed, I decided to loan it to the gallery."

"So it's not for sale?"

He shook his head. "Definitely not."

"Oh."

"Not everything in the gallery is for sale."

"How do you know the difference?"

He motioned for her to follow him back to the prior room. He approached a portrait of a lush, colorful garden with a dog hiding in a bush. Then he pointed to the bottom right corner of the frame. "See this red tag?" When she nodded, he said, "This means the piece is still available for sale."

"I understand."

"For the most part, they have the sale items together and the nonsale items in a different room."

"You seem to know a lot about the gallery."

He nodded. "I've known the owners for years. They're the reason I started the We Care Foundation."

"I don't understand."

And so he told her of Jacques and his health problems. "He was the three-year-old I mentioned earlier. His parents lost their jobs because they were caring for their son. I'd known them previously from the village and wanted to help. When they said they wanted to start their own business, I was all for it."

"So you started this art gallery for them."

He shook his head. "Definitely not. I wouldn't have had a clue of how to go about it. I just made start-up funds available to them so they could make their dreams come true. They've since paid back the loan. And now my foundation makes similar loans to other struggling families."

"That's fascinating. You're doing such amazing work that helps so many people."

"My family thinks my sole focus should be on preparations for becoming king one day."

"But you're doing that by caring for the citizens. I would think that's what a good king would want to do."

He shrugged. "When my uncle abdicated the throne, the whole country experienced unrest, from riots to staging a plot to steal the throne. I was very young then, but I remember the fear that rippled through the palace. I'd never seen my parents so scared before. At one point, we were driven from the palace in the dead of night because of security issues. We went into hiding in the countryside. My mother changed after that. She became a lot more serious, and her thoughts are always about protecting the crown."

"I didn't know that."

"Why would you?"

She was quiet for a moment. And he sensed there was something she was keeping from him.

When she didn't answer, he asked again, "Why would you know that? You're from Greece."

"I didn't see any reference to the unrest in the history book I just bought," she improvised.

He nodded in understanding. "I'm sure it's in there. You just haven't gotten to it yet."

"Your Highness, I was hoping to catch you before you left." An older woman with short dark hair and a smile that warmed her face approached them. She bowed to the prince.

"Esme, it's so good to see you." Istvan stepped forward and gave the woman a quick embrace. When he stepped back, he asked, "How is Georges?"

"He is doing good. He's at home today. He's remodeling the house. He keeps telling me it's almost done, and then he finds something else to work on." She shook her head. "As long as he's happy, I suppose I can put up with the mess. At least for a little longer."

"And how is Jacques?"

Her smile broadened. "He got a clean bill of health at his last appointment. He's growing up so quickly. He'll be sorry he didn't get to see you today, but he is helping his papa." Esme's attention turned to Indigo. "And who do we have here?"

"Esme, I'd like you to meet Indigo." His attention turned to Indi, who was wearing a friendly smile. "Indigo, I'd like you to meet the owner of this gallery, Esme Durand."

The two women greeted each other, and when Indi stuck out her hand for a handshake, Esme did what she always did—she pulled her into a hug.

When Esme pulled back, she said, "I knew when Istvan brought that sketch to the gallery that there was more to it than liking the piece of art, which, by the way, is excellent. You wouldn't believe how many offers I've had to buy it."

Color flooded Indi's cheeks. "Thank you."

Istvan nodded in agreement. "I am so impressed with her work that I've hired her to do my formal portrait."

Esme's brows rose. "That's quite an honor." Her gaze moved between the two of them. "You make such a cute couple."

"Oh, but we're not," Indi said.

"You're not a couple?" Esme looked confused.

"We're friends," Istvan offered. Though he couldn't help but think of the legend of the Ruby Heart. Were they destined to be together?

As soon as the outlandish thought came to him, he dismissed it. There wasn't a chance. Indi didn't even want to admit that the kiss they'd shared was more than a spur-of-the-moment action. But he remembered how her body had trembled with desire when he'd kissed her neck.

Ding.

His phone interrupted his errant thoughts. "I need to check this." He withdrew his phone from his pocket and read the screen. "I have a meeting at three. I'm sorry, but we need to be going."

Indi nodded. "Of course." She turned back to Esme. "Thank you for opening the gallery for us. I really enjoyed getting to stroll through it. Your pieces are beautiful."

"I hope you'll come back and bring some of your own artwork. I'd love to display it for you." Esme hugged Indi again.

As they walked away, he said, "I hope you're not upset with me for lending them my sketch."

She shook her head. "Not at all. I'm just surprised you think it's good enough to display for the public."

As they walked toward the exit, he said, "I think you are wildly talented and you are about to impress the art world with your talent."

Pink stained her cheeks. "You don't have to say that."

"I know. I said it because I meant it."

Once out on the sidewalk, he turned toward the palace, and she said, "We're walking back?"

"Is that a problem?"

"No. Uh… I just thought you were in a hurry."

"Why waste a summer afternoon? There's time to walk. And between you and me, if I'm a few minutes late for the meeting, they'll wait."

"I suppose you're right. After all, you are the crown prince." She didn't smile.

He felt as though that had come out all wrong. "I didn't mean it the way it sounded. I don't throw my position around. I just meant that I won't be more than a couple of minutes late and they would wait."

He hadn't explained that sufficiently. They continued to walk in silence. There was something about Indi that made him feel a little off-kilter. And it felt like there was something she wanted to say, but she was holding back.

They were passing by a small park on the edge of the village. Trees and bushes were strategically placed on the walkways. Sunshine poked through the leafy canopy as a gentle breeze swept past them.

He wanted to make sure things were all right between them before they reached the palace. "Let's stop here."

She glanced over at the quiet park before turning her gaze back to him. "What about your meeting?"

"This is more important."

Worry showed in her eyes. "What is it?"

He guided her to a park bench. They sat down and he turned to her. "What's wrong?"

She shrugged. "Nothing."

"That's not true. I've had the feeling something was bothering you all day. What is it?"

"I… I just didn't know that you'd decided to go with the palace's artist."

"And I explained that it's just to pacify my mother. When the formal portrait is decided, it will be yours that I choose."

"You can't say that. You haven't even seen it yet."

"No, I haven't. But I know what you're capable of, and I know you'll breathe life into the painting. You'll give my image a different perspective, and that's what I want people to see—I want them to know that when I'm king, I'll bring about change."

Whimper.

He paused and glanced around. "Did you hear that?"

"Hear what?"

"Shh… Listen."

Whimper. Whimper.

Istvan stood and glanced all around. He didn't

see an animal anywhere. Could he have imagined it?

Indi stood next to him. She too glanced around.

Not sure if he'd really heard anything, he asked, "You did hear that, didn't you?"

She nodded. "What do you think it is? Are there wild animals around here?"

"There are, but I don't think you have anything to worry about. Whatever it is sounds hurt."

Ding.

When he didn't make any move to grab his phone, Indi asked, "Don't you need to check that?"

He shook his head. "It's just another reminder about the meeting."

She nodded in understanding. "You should get going. You don't want to be late."

He didn't hear any sounds now. And he had no idea where the sound had come from, so he should return to the palace. When he turned to leave, he noticed Indi wasn't beside him. He glanced back. "You're not coming with me?"

She continued to look around. "I think I'll stay here and look for the animal."

"But what if it's a great big bear?" He raised his hands like claws and bared his teeth.

She elbowed him. "You just told me I have nothing to worry about."

Whimper. Whimper.

"There it is again," Indi said. "Can you tell where it came from?"

Istvan was already moving in the direction of the sound. He was headed straight for an overgrown bush near a tree. The closer he got, the louder the whimper became.

He honestly wasn't sure what to expect. He sure didn't want to find a bear cub, as he knew the mama wouldn't be far away. Wildlife abounded around the village and palace with the mountains in the background. But no matter what lay in the bushes, he had to attempt to help it.

Indi moved up beside him.

"What are you doing?" he asked.

"Helping."

"Get back. We don't know what we'll find."

"I'm not going anywhere. You check this side and I'll check the other side."

He watched as she moved around the bush. And then he did the same thing on his side. He stared intently into the shadows between the little leaves, but he couldn't make anything out.

"It's okay," he said in a soft voice. "I'm just going to help you."

"Istvan, over here."

He moved as fast as he could, not knowing if Indi was in trouble or not. When he rounded the giant bush, he found her down on her hands and knees, flashing the light on her phone Into a hole.

"What is it?" he asked.

"A puppy. It's trapped in the hole. Every time it tries to climb out, it falls. We have to help him."

Istvan dropped to his knees. He leaned forward and placed his hand down the hole, but he couldn't reach the puppy, who continued to whimper.

Istvan lay flat on the ground. He gently inserted his arm in the hole. His fingers moved, hoping to feel fur. Still nothing. And then there it was.

He moved his upper body, trying to lower his hand just a little farther. Just enough to wrap his fingers around the puppy's chest. *Just...a...little...farther.*

With a great big sigh, he pulled his arm back. "I can't quite reach him. I was so close."

Frustration knotted up his gut. He rolled over onto his back, expecting to see Indi, but she wasn't there. He sat up and looked around. He spotted her off in the distance.

"What are you doing?" he called out to her.

She rushed back to him with a large, flat rock in her hand. She used it to start dragging the soil away from what must be a rabbit hole, if the bits of fur surrounding the opening were any indication.

He searched around for another rock. With a rock in hand, he joined her. Together they dug at the ground, widening the opening.

He had no idea how much time had passed before he once again lay on his stomach and lowered his arm into the hole. There was no longer any whimpering. He hoped they weren't too late.

He lowered his hand into the hole. He moved slowly, not wanting to hurt the puppy or send it farther down the hole.

And then his fingers once more touched the soft fur. He gently wrapped his fingers around the pup. Very slowly he began to lift.

When the black-and-white puppy was freed, it blinked its blue eyes and stared at him with a sad look. Istvan smiled at him.

Indi ran her fingers over its back. "It's okay, little one. You're safe now." She glanced at Istvan. "What should we do with him?"

"We'll take him home. He needs water, food and a bath."

"Home? As in the palace?" She looked at him with surprise written all over her face.

"Sure. Why not? Let's go. I'll have my secretary notify someone in the village of the hole. It'll need filled in so no other animal falls in it. And I'll have them get out the news about the puppy so the owner will know where to find him."

He was so relieved to have been able to rescue the puppy. He didn't even want to think about what would have happened if he hadn't suggested they stop in the park to talk. And then he realized they hadn't quite finished their conversation.

As they walked quickly toward the palace, he asked, "Are we okay?"

Her gaze met his. "We're good."

"You're sure?"

She smiled at him. "Positive."

He expelled a small sigh of relief. One problem solved—and now another one to contend with. The puppy was docile in his arm. He hoped that wasn't a bad sign.

CHAPTER SIXTEEN

HE'D NEVER HAD a pet in his life.

And suddenly this orphaned puppy was so important to Istvan. Maybe it was because he knew how it felt to lose part of your family. His thoughts briefly strayed to his uncle—the man he'd had a closer bond with than his own father.

Maybe in part it was the fact that he could help the puppy. He could do it himself. He wanted to save the puppy and nurse it back to health. He wanted to feel needed instead of merely being a showpiece of the palace.

They entered the palace through the front door. He wasn't going to waste time walking to the side entrance, which was normal protocol unless they were welcoming guests.

Once in the foyer, Indi asked, "Have you ever had a puppy before?"

"No. But I'm sure I can figure it out." He noticed her lack of agreement. "Maybe you could help me."

She nodded. "I used to have a dog. His name was Charlie. He was big and friendly."

He was relieved to hear that at least one of them would know what they were doing. He took the stairs two at a time until he realized Indi was having problems keeping up with him. He slowed down for her. When he stopped in front of his suite, Indi rushed to open the door for him. Once they were inside, she pushed the door shut.

"He needs water." Indi turned in a circle, searching the spacious room for something to use as a water bowl.

Istvan moved to the seating area and grabbed a dish from the end table. He handed it to her. "This should do."

Indi gaped at him and then looked at the dish. "But this is an antique."

"It's a bowl." He didn't care how old the dish was as long as it held water. "You can get water in the bathroom."

She moved toward the bathroom and soon returned with a bowl of water. She set the bowl on the floor as he placed the puppy near it. When the creature didn't move to drink, Indi dipped her finger in the water and then dabbed his nose. His pink tongue came out and licked his nose. She did it again. And soon the puppy was drinking out of the bowl—in between dribbling water everywhere.

"I'll start the bath." She started toward the

bathroom. At the doorway, she paused and turned back to him. "Do you think there's some baby shampoo in the palace?"

"I don't know, but I can find out."

"What about food?"

"I'll have someone get us some puppy basics from the village."

Indi nodded in agreement before slipping into the bathroom. He placed a call to his secretary, requesting baby shampoo as well as other puppy supplies.

A couple of minutes after ending the call, there was a knock at the door. *That was really fast.*

"Come in." Istvan really didn't want to deal with another visitor. He had more important things to do. He picked up the puppy and held it close to his chest, oblivious to the dirt on its coat.

The door opened, and Gisella stepped into the room. Upon spotting the puppy, her eyes widened. "So it's true."

"If you're referring to this—" he gestured toward the dog "—then yes, I have a puppy."

His sister crossed her arms as she stared across the room. "You know Mother won't approve."

"I know." And that wasn't going to change his mind. The only way he was giving up the little guy was if his owner was located. But he didn't want to think about that now.

"What are you going to do?"

"Keep him."

His sister, being a rule follower, frowned at him. "Why do you always have to cause trouble?"

He was confused. "How is having a dog causing trouble?"

"Isn't it enough that you're the crown prince? You always seem to want more. How much is enough for you?" And with that she spun around and stormed out of the room, almost running into his other sisters.

It appeared news of the puppy had quickly made it around the palace. Beatrix and Cecilia rushed into the room, ignoring him in their excitement to fuss over the puppy, who didn't seem to mind their attention.

"Can I hold him?" Cecilia pleaded with her eyes. "Please."

Istvan shook his head. "He's too dirty."

"I don't mind." She held out her hands for the pup.

He gently handed over the puppy. "Be careful with him."

Cecilia frowned at him. "Of course."

"What are you going to name him?" Beatrix asked.

He kept his attention on the puppy. "I don't know. We haven't discussed it."

"We?" There was a singsong tone to Cecilia's voice.

He ignored his sister's insinuation. "Indi—

erm, Indigo was with me when we found him in the park."

"You just happened to be in the park together?" Beatrix looked at him expectantly, like he was going to confide some great love affair.

"It isn't like that," he said.

"Isn't it?" Cecilia asked. "We've all seen the way you look at her."

"Especially Mother and Father," Beatrix interjected. "You have them really worried."

Indi stepped back in the room. "Did I hear someone?" Her gaze landed on his sisters. "Oh, hi."

His sisters greeted her. He didn't want them to say anything further and upset Indi, so he said, "They were just leaving," and gave them a pointed look.

Once they were alone again, Indi said, "The bathtub is ready."

Knock-knock.

This time it was one of the household staff with the requested shampoo.

Istvan lifted the puppy until they were eye to eye. The puppy's blue eyes stared at him, and Istvan felt a protective feeling that he'd never experienced before. "It's okay, little fellow. We're just going to clean you up a bit. And then we'll get you fed."

He lowered the puppy to his chest as he followed Indigo into the bathroom. There were a couple of inches of warm water in the tub, and when he placed the puppy in the water, the puppy wasn't quite sure how to react.

Indi put some baby shampoo on her hands and rubbed them together to suds it up. Then she set to work washing the puppy. "You know, if you plan to keep him around, he's going to need a name."

He definitely wanted to keep the puppy, but he also had to slow down and realize that he might have a home. He might have a family that was frantically searching for him.

"Maybe we should wait on that until we post some notices in the village and see if he has owners that are searching for him."

"But we can't just keep calling him 'the puppy.'"

"Okay, what do you have in mind?"

She studied the puppy for a moment. "It should be something proper, if he's going to be a prince's dog." She paused as though sorting through names in her mind. And then her eyes widened. "I know. You could call him Duke."

Istvan's gaze moved from her to the dog and back again. His parents would have a fit over the name, but that didn't deter him. "I like it." He glanced at the pup. "What do you think, Duke? Do you like your name?"

The puppy just gave him a wide-eyed stare before he stood up and shook, showering them with soap suds. They glanced at each other and laughed.

Since Indi had come into his life, things had been changing. She was showing him that it was all right to go after what he wanted. And as he looked at her, he realized that he wanted her. But he knew it could never work—not with him here in Rydiania and her back in Greece, where her mother lived.

Where were they going?

The following evening as darkness fell over the kingdom, Indigo settled back against the leather seat of Istvan's sport utility vehicle with Duke in her lap. The puppy was in surprisingly good health. Even the veterinarian in the village had been surprised by his appetite and energy. And so far no one had claimed him. They made sure Duke was always with one or both of them, as he wasn't housebroken and they'd already had to clean up a few accidents. And then there was the fact he liked to chew on things—most especially Istvan's shoes. He definitely kept them busy.

But earlier in the day, when Istvan sat for his portrait, Duke had fallen asleep on his lap. While the other artist fussed about the dog's presence being most inappropriate, Indigo thought the scene was precious. And if the portrait hadn't needed to be proper, she would have included

Duke. The puppy gave Istvan an authentic quality. And she felt herself falling for both man and dog.

Now all three of them were off on an adventure. She had been surprised when Istvan hadn't opted to take his sports car. But she supposed if she had an entire fleet of vehicles to choose from, she would mix things up every now and then, too. Though she couldn't imagine having one sports car, much less a selection of top-of-the-line vehicles.

As Duke slept on her lap, her gaze moved to Istvan. She noticed how his long fingers wrapped around the steering wheel. Her gaze followed his muscled arms up to his broad shoulders—shoulders that she longed to lean into as his arms wrapped around her. A dreamy sigh escaped her lips.

"Did you say something?" Istvan's voice interrupted her daydream.

"Um…no." Heat swirled in her chest and rushed to her cheeks. Needing to divert the conversation, she said, "It's a beautiful sunset. With all the oranges, pinks and purples, it makes me long to pull out my paints and put it on canvas."

"Not tonight. I have something else in mind."

"But we already passed the village. Where are we going?" And then she thought about her arrival here and their drive from the airport. "Wait. Are we going into the city?"

"Perhaps. Would you like that?"

She sat up a little straighter. "I would. I mean, while I'm here, I might as well see as much as I can. Where are we having dinner?"

"It's a surprise."

Her thoughts slipped back to her dinner with the royal family. It had been so stressful that she wasn't sure if she'd even eaten, and if she had, she couldn't remember what it tasted like. She could definitely do without a surprise like that one.

Her hand moved over the puppy's soft fur. "Will any of your family be at this dinner?"

"No. Definitely not."

She breathed easier. "That's good."

It wasn't until the words were out of her mouth that she realized her thoughts had translated to her lips. The breath caught in her lungs as she waited for Istvan to respond. She hoped her slip hadn't ruined the whole evening.

"I agree. I'm really sorry about the other night. It won't happen again."

Her pent-up breath whooshed from her lungs. "It's not your fault."

"But they are my family. And if I had known my mother was going to be that way, I never would have agreed to the dinner."

The SUV slowed as it entered the city. Duke stood up on her lap and put his tiny paws on the door so he could peer out the window. The streets were busy, but the prince's escort stayed with them. One vehicle was in front and one in back.

Even if they had to run a red light, the caravan stayed together.

"I noticed you're able to move about the village without your escort, but not so much in the city."

"Don't let them fool you. I always have protection. The risk in the city is a lot higher. I can't move about here without bodyguards next to me."

"That must be rough. I can't even imagine what it's like having people watching my every move."

He shrugged. "You'd be surprised what you can get used to. But where we're going, we'll have some privacy."

"That's good, because I doubt many restaurants are going to be happy when we walk in with Duke."

Istvan reached over and petted the puppy. "You never know. He might win them all over."

"You mean like he did with us?"

Istvan smiled. "Exactly."

Woof-woof.

They both laughed at Duke's agreement.

They made their way into the heart of the city. She couldn't help but wonder where the art district might be. She'd love to visit it. But then again, she didn't even know what Istvan had planned for this evening. She just hoped her dress would be appropriate.

She'd chosen one of the dresses that had been delivered to her room the evening before. This time she'd selected a midnight-blue lace minidress. Its stretchy material fit snugly against her hips and waist. Her arms and shoulders were bared by the halter neckline. She'd matched it with her heeled sandals.

"Are you sure you won't tell me what you have planned?" she asked, not that there was anything she could do about her outfit now.

"No. But we're almost there."

The vehicle slowed as the lead car put on its turn signal. They were turning into an underground garage. Interesting.

They parked, and then they stepped into an elevator with two of his security detail. A key-card swipe and a button push had them heading for the top floor. Since she didn't know what kind of building this was, she didn't know what would be up there. She could only assume it was a restaurant with a beautiful view.

The doors whooshed open. They stepped out into a nondescript hallway, and as she glanced around, she noticed there were four doors, numbered one through four. Istvan started for the door with a gold number one on it.

Istvan opened the door and then turned back to her. "Come in."

With Duke in her arms, she passed by him. She got the slightest whiff of his spicy cologne, and for the briefest moment, she considered stopping and leaning in close to him to breathe in that most intoxicating scent, but as quickly as the thought came to her, she dismissed it. She had to keep her wits about her. Letting herself fall for the prince would lead to nothing but heartache.

She didn't know what she expected to find when she stepped through the door. Instead of a sparse modern apartment, she found skylights and greenery. There were plants throughout the large, open room.

She turned back to him as he stood near the now-closed door. "Where are we?"

"This is my new penthouse. I had it completely remodeled."

"It's amazing." Her gaze moved back to the two large couches and handful of comfortable-looking chairs. "It's nothing like the palace."

"No. It's not. And that's the way I like it."

"I didn't know you liked plants this much." Duke began to squirm in her arms.

"I like being outdoors. So I thought I'd bring the outdoors inside."

"Do you mind if I put Duke down to explore?"

"Not at all. I had them stock the apartment with puppy supplies. Where I go, he will go."

She released Duke's leash and then put him on the floor. While the puppy explored, she walked around the room taking in all the details, from the hanging plants to the marble animal statues. Even with so many plants in the room, it still didn't feel crowded. There was plenty of room for a party or just for Istvan to kick back on the couch and enjoy his gigantic television. And off to the side was a modern kitchen that looked as though it had never been used.

In the corner of the kitchen were silver bowls with Duke's name on them. And next to the couch was a box of puppy toys. Indigo smiled. Even when she was gone, she knew Duke would be well cared for and loved. Istvan would see to it.

"How long have you had this place?" She moved toward the wall of windows.

"The remodel was just completed. I've never actually stayed here. In fact, you are my first guest."

She ignored the way her heart fluttered in her chest. She turned to him and found him approaching her. "Thank you for sharing this with me."

"I'm happy to have you here. Please, sit down."

She sat on the couch and found that not only was it nice-looking but it was also comfortable. When Istvan sat in one of the chairs, there was an air of relaxation about him. The worry lines smoothed from his face, and he looked so at home.

She reached into her oversize purse and withdrew a small sketch pad and pencil. She couldn't resist capturing this moment. And though she knew she could easily snap a photo of him on her phone, it just wouldn't be the same.

"What are you doing?" he asked.

She flipped open the sketchbook, and soon she

was moving the pencil over the paper in rapid movements. "I just want to capture this moment."

"Wouldn't you rather eat? I have dinner planned for us out on the balcony."

"In just a moment." Luckily, she was quite skilled with sketches, so this wouldn't take long.

She couldn't pass up the peacefulness written all over his face. He never looked like this when they were within the palace walls. This place was good for him. She was glad he'd found a home away from home.

And this sketch was for herself. With only three more days in Rydiania, their time together was drawing to a close. She wanted something to remember him by—the real Istvan, the man who wasn't bothered by getting dirty to save a puppy, who didn't yell when his dress shoes had tiny bite marks.

That wasn't the man she'd expected to find within the palace walls. He also wasn't the man she'd expected to break through the wall around her heart. He was a man of many surprises.

CHAPTER SEVENTEEN

DINNER WAS DELICIOUS.

The company was divine.

And Duke had worn himself out exploring the penthouse and had fallen asleep in his new bed, giving them some alone time.

The meal had been served out on the balcony. Istvan smiled across the candlelit table at Indi. She seemed to enjoy the food, though he noticed she didn't eat it all.

"Was everything to your expectations?" he asked.

"The meal was delicious. There was just so much of it."

She got to her feet, reached for her wineglass and then moved to the edge of the balcony. He joined her there. Quietly they watched as the last lingering rays of the sun sank below the horizon.

She turned to him. "You have such a beautiful view."

He gazed deep into her eyes. "I couldn't agree more." But it wasn't the sunset he had on his mind. He reached out to her. The backs of his fingers brushed over her cheek. "Indi, I—"

"We should go inside." She jumped back as though his touch had shocked her. "It's getting cool out."

Really? Because he thought it was rather warm. But he didn't argue the point as he followed her inside.

Once inside, Indi moved to the sectional sofa with deep red cushions while he checked on Duke, who lifted his head, yawned and then went back to sleep. Istvan joined Indi on the couch. He still felt as though the disastrous meal with his parents was standing between them, like a wall that he wasn't able to scale.

But he refused to give up the idea of bridging the gap. There had to be something he could say, something he could do, something that would recreate the closeness they'd once shared.

He turned to her. "Indigo, talk to me."

Her gaze met his, but her thoughts were hidden behind a blank stare. "What do you want to talk about?"

He realized that it was up to him to start this conversation. "I'm sorry things haven't gone well with my family."

"Stop apologizing. I don't hold it against you. And, by the way, I really like your sisters."

"You do?" When she nodded, he said, "Gisella can be a little intense."

"That's just because she cares about you."

"So if it's not my family, why do I feel like you keep putting walls between us?"

She turned her head and gazed into his eyes. "Are you happy?"

She was avoiding his questions. He shrugged. "I don't know."

"That's not a very positive response."

He suddenly felt uncomfortable with the direction of this conversation. No one had ever asked him that. "I've never allowed myself to consider the question. My future was mapped out for me even before I was born."

"You don't have to do it. You don't have to become the king—not if it won't make you happy."

He sat up straighter and stared at her. "Are you telling me to walk away from the crown?"

"Of course not. I'm telling you not to make yourself miserable. Find a way to be happy, whether it's here at your penthouse or inside the palace walls. If you aren't happy with your choices, you won't be of any help to those around you."

He'd never thought of it that way. But he did know one thing that made him happy. He gazed at Indi. His gaze dipped to her lips before moving back to her eyes, which reflected her own desire.

"Kissing you would make me happy." He leaned in close to her and claimed her lips with his own. Her kiss was sweet, like the wine they'd been drinking. And it was so much more intoxicating.

He knew this moment—this night—wouldn't be enough time with Indigo. He didn't know how he'd do it, but he wanted to see her after this week. There had to be a way to get her to stay here in Rydiania.

When his arms wrapped around her to draw her close, her hands pressed on his chest. And then, to his great disappointment, she pulled away from him.

"This…" She gestured between the two of them. "It can't happen."

He expelled a frustrated sigh. "There you go again putting up a wall between us. Why do you keep fighting the inevitable?"

"Because your family has a habit of getting rid of the people that don't fall in line with their expectations." She said it so matter-of-factly that it caught him off guard.

"What?" And then he realized what she was referring to. "You mean the way they treated my uncle."

A frown pulled at her face. "It wasn't just your uncle. There were a lot of other people that got hurt when your parents threw them out of the country—expelled them from the only homes they'd ever known."

He was surprised by her level of emotion about something that had happened when they were nothing more than kids. "You must have learned a lot about my uncle while reading that book you bought in the village."

"I didn't learn any of this from a book." Her voice was soft and held a note of…what was it? Was that pain he detected?

As the darkness closed in around them, he longed to be able to look into her eyes. "Indi, tell me what's going on." He reached out, taking her hand in his. "What don't I know?"

Her gaze searched his. "You really don't know, do you?"

"No. Or I wouldn't have asked."

She paused as though gathering her thoughts. "I'm Rydianian."

He was confused. "But you're from Greece."

"We moved to Greece when I was very young. But I was born in the village that you love so much."

And suddenly the pieces fell into place. "That's why you wanted to find the village square."

She nodded. "Our home was in the square overlooking the fountain."

"Why didn't you tell me before now?"

"At first I thought you knew exactly who I was from the background check. By the time I realized that you didn't know, we were already here, and I couldn't afford to lose the contract. I'd already spent the money to get my mother into an assisted living unit."

"Whoa! Slow down." He had the feeling he was still missing something big. "Why would I have fired you if I knew you were born here?"

Her gaze lowered. "Because of who my father was."

A cold chill came over him. "Who was your father?"

Her gaze rose to meet his. Unshed tears shimmered in her eyes. "He was King Georgios's private secretary. When your uncle was banished from the kingdom, so was my father. He lost everything."

Istvan got to his feet and moved to the window. He combed his fingers through his hair as he digested this news. Never again would he read just the highlights of a background check. He suddenly felt like he understood Indi so much better and why she kept putting up barriers between them.

"I'm sorry I didn't tell you sooner." The soft lilt of her voice came from right behind him.

A rush of emotions plowed into him. Anger at her for keeping this from him, anger at himself for not pushing harder when he sensed she was keeping something from him, anger at his parents for wrecking more lives in order to preserve the crown. And then there was sympathy, because he, too, had had his young life turned upside down when his favorite uncle was gone with no explanation and he was forbidden to speak of him.

And then he realized how hard it must have been for Indi to come to Rydiania and then to face the king and queen. He couldn't imagine what that must have been like for her, but he knew what strength it took. He admired her more than he ever had before.

He turned to her. "I'm sorry for what you and your family endured."

The apology was small in light of the magnitude of the damage that had been done. He longed to reach out to her and pull her close, but he hesitated, not wanting her to pull away again.

Her pain-filled gaze met his. "You don't have to apologize. You did nothing wrong. You were just a child at the time."

"Your family moved to Greece?"

Indi nodded. "My mother had some distant relatives there. My father, well, he never liked it there. He was never the same after we left Rydiania. He started to drink. And then one day when I was a teenager…" Her voice trailed away as tears slipped down her cheeks. "I…"

He heard the pain in her voice from dredging up these memories. "It's okay. We don't have to talk about this."

This time he did pull her into his embrace. He wanted to absorb all her pain and agony. In that moment, he would have done anything to make her feel better, but there was nothing he could do but stand there and hold her. He'd never felt so helpless.

Indi pulled back and swiped at her damp cheeks. "I came home and found he'd killed himself." Fresh tears splashed onto her cheeks. When she spoke her voice was rough with emotion. "When he was banished from the palace, from the life of service that had been passed down to him from his parents and grandparents, he lost a piece of himself. He...he was never whole again. It broke my mother to watch the man she loved disintegrate before her eyes, and there was nothing she could do. I can't imagine loving someone that much and then feeling so helpless."

"I'm so sorry."

She gazed at him with bloodshot eyes and tearstained cheeks that tore at his heart. "You lost someone you loved, too."

Even in her moment of great pain, she was able to offer compassion. He was in awe of her. She was the kind of queen Rydiania needed, but now he knew there was absolutely no chance of that ever happening.

He wrapped his arms around her, wanting to protect her from the pain, the horrific memories and even from his parents. They could never find out about Indi's past, because if they did, they'd banish her—the same thing they'd done to her father—in order to keep them apart.

When Indi lifted her head to look at him, he

dipped his head to reclaim her lips. Her arms snaked their way around his neck, pulling him closer.

He'd never felt so close to a person. Now that the wall was gone between them, he didn't want to let her go. He wanted to make the most of this night.

This time he was the one to pull back. "Indi, stay here with me."

"You still want me after everything I told you?"

"I do. More than ever. But do you want me?"

She immediately nodded, and desire flared in her eyes. "I do."

He swung her up in his arms and carried her down the hallway to his room. He moved to the king-size bed.

He gazed down at her—wanting her so very much. "Are you sure?"

"I am." She reached out, hooking her fingers through the belt loops on his pants, and pulled him toward her.

Once he was next to her, she pressed her lips to his. This was going to be a night neither of them would ever forget.

CHAPTER EIGHTEEN

THIS PROJECT WAS going better than she'd imagined. In fact, she was enjoying herself a lot.

Since last night, she couldn't stop smiling. She couldn't prevent what was going to happen in the future, but she could savor each moment she had left with Istvan. Even though it was already Wednesday and her plane was to take off on Friday evening, she intended to make the most of the time they had left.

Istvan had been so sweet and caring after she told him about her past. She had finally decided that he was nothing like his parents, or at least he hadn't given in to those unsavory traits.

When he'd held her and kissed her, he'd revealed to her the vulnerable side of himself. She was glad he had the penthouse, where he could escape and just be himself.

She lifted her gaze from the portrait, where she'd begun to paint his image. She intended to give him an approachable expression—one that hinted at his vulnerabilities but also showed his strength. It would be her greatest piece of work.

Indigo sat on a stool in front of the canvas. She glanced past the easel to Istvan, who sat casually in the armchair next to the window with the sunshine streaming in. He was her favorite subject ever.

Woof-woof.

Duke had decided he'd been held quite enough. He was busy chewing and chasing his toys about the big open floor.

Every time the puppy made a noise, the artist next to her would let out a disgusted sigh. How could anyone dislike a puppy? Especially when one was as cute and loving as Duke.

When they'd arrived at the palace that morning, Istvan's secretary had told him that Duke's owners had been located. The family was honored that their dog's puppy had become part of the royal family. She'd seen the relief in Istvan's eyes when he learned that Duke was officially his, and she'd been happy for both of them.

She continued to work, excited to see the final product, because try as she might, the finished portrait was never exactly how she initially envisioned it. Sometimes it was better, sometimes not. Then her gaze moved to the older man, who frowned as his hand moved rapidly over his canvas. He was very focused. Yet when he found her staring at him, he glanced over at her with a scowl. *Yikes.* Talk about a man feeling insecure about his abilities. If he was comfortable with his skills, he wouldn't care that she was there.

"I need a break." Istvan stood and stretched. "We'll pick this back up this afternoon."

The other artist continued to work while she put down her pencil. She lowered the cloth over the canvas to keep Istvan from sneaking a look. There was nothing about this piece that she was ready to share with anyone.

She glanced over the canvas to see Istvan gesturing to her to join him. She was more than happy to spend some more one-on-one time with him. After their night at his penthouse, she felt closer to him than she had any other man in her life.

"I was thinking we should take Duke for a walk in the garden," he said. "What do you think?"

"I think that would be lovely." Then she lowered her voice. "But what about him?" She gestured over her shoulder to the other artist.

Istvan whispered in her ear, "I think he has plenty to work with."

"Perhaps you're right." As they made their way into the hallway, she asked, "How about we have a picnic lunch in the garden? We can soak up some sunshine while Duke runs around."

"I think it's a great idea. I'll have the kitchen pack up a lunch." He reached for his phone and placed a quick call. When he put his phone in his pocket, he said, "It's all been arranged."

"Thank you." She was tempted to kiss him, but she refrained, as they'd both agreed to avoid any public displays of affection around the palace. Why did life have to be so complicated?

It was a perfect summer afternoon.

But Indigo was what made the day all bright and shiny.

Istvan wasn't ready for this picnic lunch to end. Even Duke had run around and barked so much that he'd worn himself out. He was now stretched out against Istvan's legs taking a puppy nap.

Everything had changed between him and Indi last night. And it was so much more than their lovemaking. They'd learned to trust each other with everything. He'd even dare to say she was the closest friend he'd ever had, but he knew that wasn't a fair assessment, because they were so much more than friends...though he wasn't ready to put a label on it. He just wanted to enjoy it as long as he could.

Ding.

He sighed. "I'm beginning to hate that sound."

"Just change the ringtone." Indi gathered the leftovers.

"No. I mean, I hate that it reminds me that I have obligations when all I want to do is stay here with you." He glanced around to see if anyone was watching. When he didn't see anyone, he gently grabbed her wrist and slowly drew her to him.

"Istvan, what are you doing?" There was a playful smile on her lips. "We agreed on no public displays of affection."

"But there's no one around." He pressed his lips to hers. This was what he would think of on future summer afternoons. Because in this moment with Indi and Duke, life was perfect. He was fulfilled.

Ding.

He groaned as Indi pulled away. She let out a sweet and melodious laugh.

"How can you laugh?" he asked with a frown. "It's not fair that I'm being drawn away from this to go sit in some tedious meeting."

"It's not that bad." She smiled at him as he continued to frown.

"Yes, it is. And it's your fault."

"My fault?" She pressed a hand to her chest.

"Yes. You showed me what I could be doing, and now my business pales in comparison."

She let out another laugh. Her eyes twinkled with happiness. "Well, I'm sorry if I did all that."

"You should be." And then he leaned forward and stole another quick kiss. When he pulled away, he said, "I needed something to tide me over until this evening."

She arched a brow. "Who says you are going to get more of that later?"

He sent her a pouting look. "You wouldn't deny me such pleasure, would you?"

She pursed her lips as though considering his plea. "I suppose not, but we have to go. Now."

With great regret that their leisurely lunch had to end, he helped her collect the remaining things. Then the three of them headed back into the palace. He hoped he didn't have to make any important decisions that afternoon, because his mind would be elsewhere as he counted down the minutes until he could see Indi again. In the meantime, Duke would keep her company.

CHAPTER NINETEEN

Her feet weren't even touching the floor.

Indigo smiled brightly as they entered the palace. It seemed so dark inside compared to the sunny gardens with their radiant blooms. She'd previously done some sketches and snapped photos of the garden so she could do some paintings when she got home.

Duke wiggled in her arms. Now that he was well-fed, he was a ball of energy. But they'd agreed it was best to carry him through the main parts of the palace where they would likely run into the king or queen.

They'd almost reached the stairs when the queen called out to them. "Can I see you both in the library?"

It wasn't so much a question as an order. Indigo inwardly groaned. The very last thing she wanted to do now was to make nice with the queen. But as Istvan sighed and turned, she did the same.

Once they were inside the library, the queen turned to one of the house staff that had just brought her a cup of tea and said, "Would you leave us? And close the door on the way out."

The older woman quietly nodded and did as she was bidden.

The queen was unusually quiet, and that worried Indigo. She was probably going to complain about Duke running through her flower gardens and trampling a few low-lying stems. As though he sensed he was in trouble, the dog settled in her arms.

The queen looked pointedly at Istvan. "Do you know who this would-be painter is?"

"I know everything I need to know about Indi."

The queen's eyes momentarily widened at his use of the nickname. "I don't think you do, or you wouldn't be rolling around in the garden with her."

Indigo gasped. They had been spied upon. She felt invaded that someone would try to ruin a private moment between her and Istvan.

"We weren't rolling around." Istvan's voice took on an angry tone.

"Regardless, she's been lying about who she is."

"I know who she is," Istvan said calmly.

"No, you don't. Her father was banished from the kingdom."

"I know." Istvan's body tensed as though he were in a struggle with himself to hold back his anger.

This time it was the queen who gasped. "But how could you spend the night with her? You are putting the crown at risk by getting involved with her. You are a prince. She is no one."

Indigo now knew what it felt like to be invisible. But she had something to say. She stepped forward.

"The prince isn't putting anything at risk," Indigo said in a steady voice, though she felt anything but steady on the inside. "We are friends. Your son never led me to believe it would be anything more. And I would never make trouble for him."

The queen gave her a stony look. "If you came here hoping for some sort of revenge—"

"Mother, stop. You are insulting Indigo and making yourself look petty in the process."

Della's eyes narrowed. "Istvan, I suggest you remember that you are speaking to the queen."

The two stared at each other as though waiting for the other to blink. Indigo felt bad that she was responsible for creating this turmoil between Istvan and his mother. She needed to do something to help him.

"I am going back to Greece," she uttered. "Today."

This ended the stare-off between the two as they both looked in her direction. There was a gleam of victory in the queen's eyes while there was sadness in Istvan's.

"I'll make the private jet available," the queen said.

It was on the tip of Indigo's tongue to thank

her, because her parents had raised her to have manners, but she decided the queen wasn't worthy of manners, not when she was so willing to hurt her son.

"Don't do this," Istvan said.

Knock-knock.

"Come," the queen said.

It was Istvan's private secretary. He bowed. "Pardon, ma'am. The king has sent me. The prince is late for a meeting."

This was Indigo's cue to make her exit. She headed for the hallway. Istvan rushed to catch up to her. He fell in step with her.

"Don't you have a meeting to attend?" she asked.

"I can't go to it until I'm sure you aren't leaving."

"It's for the best."

He didn't say another word until they reached his suite, where Duke's belongings were, including his kennel. She placed the puppy inside, and he moved to his puffy blue bed. Once Duke was secure, she straightened.

She sensed Istvan standing beside her. She wished he'd just go to his meeting and not make this more difficult. Because she had absolutely no idea how she was going to say goodbye to him. Especially now that she'd fallen head over heels in love with him.

Ding.

Ding.

Ding.

Istvan sighed. "This is important business or I wouldn't leave. Just wait for me and we can discuss it."

And then he leaned in and kissed her. Her heart lodged in her throat, as she knew this would be their final kiss. Because every fairy tale had an ending, and this was theirs.

The meeting took forever.

But in the end, an agreement was reached with the local farmers. And life would continue in the kingdom as it always had.

Istvan rushed to his suite, hoping to find Indi there playing with Duke, but the puppy was still in his crate playing with a stuffed fish. He immediately dropped it upon spotting Istvan. He barked to be let out.

Istvan paused long enough to fuss over the pup quickly and put on his leash. It was time for him to be walked. They moved down the hallway to get Indi for the walk.

Knock-knock.

"Indi?"

He knocked again, with no response. As an uneasy feeling settled in his gut, he opened the door. The dresser was devoid of Indi's sketch pads.

No. No. No.

His whole body tensed as he rushed over to the

wardrobe and swung the doors open. The only clothes inside were the dresses he'd bought her. Everything else was gone. Indi was gone.

It felt as though the air had been sucked out of the room. He stumbled over to the bed and sank down.

Why didn't she wait? Why?

"Istvan?" It was Gisella's voice.

He scrubbed his palms across his eyes and drew in a deep breath, hoping when he spoke that his voice wouldn't betray him.

"What do you need?" He kept his back to her as he bent over and picked up Duke.

"I heard about Indigo." He waited for her to agree with their mother about Indigo being trouble, but instead his sister said, "I'm sorry. But you know it has to be this way."

He turned to her. "Does it have to be this way?" He shook his head. "I don't think so."

"What are you saying?" Concern laced her voice.

"Would you be happy if the only thing you had in your life was the crown?"

"Of course." There was sincerity in her words.

He lacked that conviction. He'd always believed there were more important things in life than being crowned king. Indi was one of those things.

"How can it be enough for you?" He felt he was missing something.

"How can it not be enough?" She studied him as though she were concerned about him.

"Maybe the problem is that you should be the heir."

"I wish." And then she glanced down at the envelope in her hand. She held it out to him. "Indigo left this for you."

On wooden legs, he approached his sister. He wasn't sure he wanted to know what the note said, but he couldn't help himself.

He accepted the envelope, and his sister moved on. He slipped his finger under the flap and yanked, withdrawing the slip of paper.

I'm sorry I couldn't wait. I knew if I saw you again that you would talk me out of leaving. Your mother was right about one thing—you are the crown prince. You have to focus on the future. You will be the best king ever. The people of Rydiania need you. I will never forget our time together, but we both must move on. Me with my gallery showing and you with your need to help others. I wish you all the best.
   Indi XOX
   PS Kiss Duke for me
   PSS I'll send you money for the dress.

After reading her letter, he was certain of one thing—his future was with Indi. He didn't care what it cost him. They would be together again. Because he loved her. He'd loved her since the first time she'd sketched him. He couldn't imagine his life without her.

CHAPTER TWENTY

LIFE HAD CHANGED.

She had changed.

Indigo had been home for a few days, and nothing felt the same. Her mother had just moved into the assisted care facility, and she was happy that her mother was finally where she wanted to be. And when her mother inquired about Indigo's melancholy mood, she blamed it on jet lag and the fact that she was going to miss her mother. Neither was a lie.

She hadn't had the heart to work on the portrait of Istvan since she'd been home. She knew she couldn't put it off forever, though. Istvan had wired the remainder of her fee the day after she left Rydiania. Was that his way of cutting ties with her?

She wasn't sure. But she'd kind of been hoping for a phone call from him, and none had come. It was really over. The thought weighed heavy on her mind.

But not tonight.

Tonight was her long-awaited gallery showing. She was so excited.

She'd opted to wear the blue dress from her night in the city with Istvan. It was the only dress she'd taken that he'd given her. And she'd already sent him the money for it, but without a price tag, she'd had to guess at the value.

"Are you enjoying yourself?" her agent, Franco, asked her.

She nodded. "It's great. How did you get the press to show up?"

"I didn't. I thought you arranged it."

She shook her head. "It wasn't me."

"Well, however they found out, it's a good thing. By tomorrow, everyone in Athens will know your name. And it's only up from there."

Franco got a little overexcited at times, but she appreciated his enthusiasm. She wouldn't be a household name like Jackson Pollock or Georgia O'Keeffe, but if her name became known in the art world, her dreams would be achieved.

Suddenly there was a commotion near the front of the gallery. Flashes lit up, and excitement moved over the crowd.

"What's going on?" she asked Franco.

"It seems a celebrity has shown up."

"Who?"

"I don't know. I sent out some invites but didn't hear anything back."

And then the crowd parted and Istvan was

there, larger than life in a dark suit with a white dress shirt sans the tie, but he was accessorized by the sweetest puppy in his arms. Her heart pounded. What were they doing here?

"Duke!" Indigo rushed forward and fussed over the pup, who licked her face in return.

"Don't I rate a greeting?" Istvan asked.

A hush fell over the room as cell phones were pulled out to film the moment. Inwardly Indigo groaned. Why was he here in public with her when he knew it would stir up trouble for him?

She forced a nervous smile and then did something she'd never done before. She bowed. "Welcome, Your Highness."

"Indi, you don't need to do that," he said softly.

"I do," she whispered. And she straightened. "May I show you around?"

He nodded. "I'd like that."

And so she walked with him through the gallery. All the while she wondered what he was doing in Greece. She knew what she wanted him to say to her, but she also realized it was an impossibility. As they moved agonizingly slowly through the gallery, all she could think about was getting him alone so they could speak frankly.

When they neared the office, she signaled for him to follow her. Her heart pitter-pattered. He was so close and yet so far away.

When the door closed, she asked, "Can I hold Duke?"

He handed the puppy over.

With the dog in her arms, it kept her from reaching out to him like she longed to do. She ached to feel his kiss again, but she knew that was all in the past.

"You shouldn't be here," she said as the puppy wiggled.

"There's no other place I'd rather be." He stepped closer to her and took Duke from her. Once the puppy was on the floor, Istvan stared deep into her eyes. "I've missed you."

Her heart thumped so loudly it echoed in her ears. "I… I missed you, too. But you shouldn't be here. The press is going to make a big deal of this."

"Let them. I don't care."

He was talking nonsense. "Of course you care. You have to care. You're a prince. And not just any prince, but the crown prince. You can't just walk away from that."

He stepped closer, wrapping his hands around her waist. "I can and I did."

She shook her head, unable to accept the gravity of the words he spoke. Maybe she'd misheard him over the pounding of her heart. "Istvan, this—" she gestured between them "—isn't going to work out. You have your life, and I have mine."

"That's where you are wrong. Because where you go, I will go."

"You can't." How was he not hearing her?

"Can you look into my eyes and tell me that you don't love me?"

Really? This was what it was going to take to make him see reason—to realize that their future wasn't together. But when she stared into his bottomless eyes, she saw the future—their future.

No. No. No. She couldn't let this happen. She couldn't let him give up his future, his destiny, his family. He couldn't sacrifice all that for her.

"You can't do this." Her voice wavered.

"Yes, I can. Don't you understand that without you, I am nothing?"

"Without me, you're a prince—the future ruler of Rydiania."

"I'd much rather be the prince of your heart."

She swooned just a bit. He was saying all the right things. How was she supposed to reason with him when he was being impossibly sweet?

"Istvan, please, be reasonable. What are you going to do if you aren't a prince?" The thought of him being anything but a royal totally escaped her.

He frowned at her. "Do you think I have no other skills?"

"I, uh…" Heat engulfed her cheeks. "Of course you do. I didn't mean it that way. I'm just, well… I'm caught off guard."

The smile returned to his perfectly kissable lips. "Indigo, it is done."

"What is?" Her voice was barely more than a whisper.

"I have stepped down as heir to the throne. Gisella is going to be the future queen. She always should have been the heir. She believes the crown comes first—above all else."

Indigo couldn't believe what she was hearing. She went to step back and ended up stumbling over her own feet. Her entire body was in shock.

Why was he saying all this? What did it all mean? Why would he do this? The questions swirled in her mind at a dizzying pace.

Istvan wordlessly helped her over to the desk. When she turned to look at him, she noticed a calm serenity in his eyes. He was at peace with this decision.

"You can't do this," she begged. "Go back. Tell them you had a moment of delusion and you didn't mean any of it."

He shook his head. "I can't do that."

"Why not?"

"Because I meant every single word I said before I departed that palace."

Her mouth gaped. This couldn't be happening. She had to be imagining the entire conversation. Yes, that was it. This was nothing more than a dream. When she woke up, all would be back the way it should be—with Istvan at the palace and her at her apartment.

"Indigo, did you hear me?"

She pressed her lips together and nodded. "But you can't give up your family for me. You'll regret it, and I couldn't live with the guilt."

"Indi, relax. I'm still a part of the family."

"You are?" She was relieved but confused.

He nodded. "Because I wasn't crowned, there was no need to banish me. By royal decree, I was removed from the line of succession."

"But you're still a prince?"

"I am."

"Thank goodness. I didn't want you to end up like my father or your uncle."

"Not a chance, with you in my life."

"But why would you do this?"

"Because I love you—I love the person you are, and I like the person I am when I'm around you. So unless you can tell me that you don't love me, I plan to be wherever you go."

Happy tears blurred her vision. She blinked them away. "And if I tell you that I don't love you?"

"Then I will take my broken heart and go live like a hermit in a hut on the top of a mountain."

She smiled and shook her head. "I can't see that happening."

"Neither can I, because I love you, Indigo, and I know you love me, too."

The happy tears returned and splashed onto her cheeks. "I do love you."

As he drew nearer to her, she knew in her heart

that this union was right for them. Because she was a better person with him in her life. And now that she'd had a glimpse of the love and happiness they could have together, she couldn't imagine her life without him in it. He was the prince of her heart, now and always.

EPILOGUE

Ludus Island, September

THE LAST FEW months must have been a dream.

There was no way reality could be this good.

Indigo felt as though she was walking on clouds. After her gallery showing, her artwork had been selling as fast as she could produce it. And the amount the pieces were selling for was more than she'd ever imagined. It was enough to guarantee her mother would be able to stay in her assisted living apartment indefinitely.

With Istvan's portrait complete and hanging in the palace, Indigo was working on pieces for a new gallery showing. This time, with the help of her agent, she'd been able to land a spot in Paris. Every time she thought of how far her career had come, butterflies fluttered in her stomach.

Then there was the fact that she had her very own Prince Charming. How lucky could a girl get?

Ever since Istvan had removed himself from the line of succession, the king and queen had started changing their ways. Not only was Istvan still part of the family, but they'd welcomed Indigo as well. It wasn't a warm, fuzzy relationship, but the hostility was gone, and now she could visit the village where she'd been born without worrying that it would cause problems for Istvan.

These days Istvan split his time between Ludus Island, where he had a long-term suite at the resort, and his penthouse back in Rydiania. She was hoping that soon they could spend more time together, because she missed him when he was gone, but she had her mother here in Greece and she wanted to be close to her.

Istvan had texted her earlier that day and asked her to meet him at the resort, yet when she arrived at his suite, he wasn't there. When she texted him, he asked her to meet him out on the patio. She wondered what he was doing out there at this hour.

When she reached the doors that led outside, Istvan was standing on the patio waiting for her. "Hello, beautiful."

"Hello yourself." She rushed to him, lifted up on her tiptoes and pressed her lips to his. She'd never grow tired of his kisses. Much too soon, she pulled away. "So what are we doing here?"

"I have something to show you."

"You want to show me something out there? In the dark?"

He smiled at her, making her heart flutter in

her chest. He took her hand in his as they started to walk. "Have I told you how much I've missed you?"

She gazed into his eyes. "Not as much as I've missed you."

The still-warm sea breeze brushed softly over her skin. There were a few couples lingering and enjoying the sunset. She had to admit that the sky was worthy of a painting.

She glanced at him. "Did you want to watch the sunset?"

"Yes. But not here. I have something else in mind." He continued walking across the patio and down the steps to the lit walkway that led to the beach.

He was acting very mysterious tonight. And she was dying to know what he was up to. She didn't have to wonder for long, because soon the beach came into view. With a vibrant orange, pink and purple sunset in the background, there were votives on the beach. Their flickering lights spelled out Marry Me.

Indigo gasped as happy tears blurred her vision.

When she turned to Istvan, he dropped down on one knee. "Indigo, I knew there was something special about you from the first day we met."

"But I don't even remember speaking to you. I was so caught off guard by your presence."

"You didn't have to say a word. It was just your presence that made me curious to know more about you."

She smiled at him. "So it wasn't just coincidence that you ended up at my umbrella for a sketch?"

"Definitely not. I made sure to inquire about you."

She smiled. "You did, huh?"

"Oh, yeah. I wasn't letting you get away."

"I think you're rewriting history. All you wanted from me was my artistic skills."

"That's what I wanted you to believe. And for a while, I tried to tell myself that, too. But there was no denying the way you made me feel. You gave me the courage to go after what I wanted— the life I wanted. And I want to share that life with you."

He withdrew a ring box from his pocket and held it out to her. "Indigo, you have shown me that love is accepting and tolerant. You've helped me find the courage to step out of the destiny I was born into to create the destiny I desire. I love you, and I can't imagine my life without you in it. Will you be my princess?"

She blinked repeatedly, but it was too late. The happy tears cascaded down her cheeks. "Yes. Yes, I will."

He straightened and then slipped the diamond solitaire ring adorned with heart-shaped red rubies on her finger. As soon as she saw the ring, she realized what he'd done.

"So you believe in the legend of the Ruby Heart, huh?" she asked.

He shrugged. "Seemed to work for us. And from what I heard, it worked for Hermione and Atlas."

As she admired the ring, she said, "I wonder who will fall under the spell of the Ruby Heart next."

"I don't know, but if they are as happy as we are, they'll be the lucky ones." He wrapped his arms around her waist and pulled her close.

"How happy are you?"

"Let me show you." He lowered his head, claiming her lips.

Fairy tales really did come true.

* * * * *

*Look out for the next story in the
Greek Paradise Escape trilogy*

Coming soon!

*And if you enjoyed this story, check out these
other great reads from
Jennifer Faye*

Greek Heir to Claim Her Heart
Falling for Her Convenient Groom
Bound by a Ring and a Secret

All available now!